AN UNWITTING DISCIPLE

MARIANNE HOBBS

Scripture quotations are from the New Revised Standard Version Bible, copyright © 1989 National Council of the Churches of Christ in the United States of America. Used by permission. All rights reserved worldwide. Scriptures marked (GNT) are from the Good News Bible © 1994 published by the British and Foreign Bible Society. Good News Bible © American Bible Society 1966, 1971, 1976, 1992. Used with permission.

This is a work of fiction. Names, characters, places and incidents either are the product of the author's imagination or are used fictitiously, and any resemblance to actual persons, living or dead, businesses, companies, events, or locales is entirely coincidental.

ISBN: 978-1-4866-2700-4
eBook ISBN: 978-1-4866-2701-1

Word Alive Press
119 De Baets Street Winnipeg, MB R2J 3R9
www.wordalivepress.ca

WORD ALIVE
—P R E S S—

Cataloguing in Publication information can be obtained from Library and Archives Canada.

*This book is dedicated to all those who took the time
to not only read but offer helpful, much-appreciated suggestions.*

Then Pilate handed Jesus over to them to be crucified.

So they took charge of Jesus. He went out, carrying his cross, and came to "The Place of the Skull," as it is called. (In Hebrew it is called "Golgotha.") There they crucified him; and they also crucified two other men, one on each side, with Jesus between them. (John 19:16–18, GNT)

PROLOGUE

Had I caused this? Was I, through my words, responsible? Could I have tried harder to stop it? Guilt suffocated me, but it was the Rabbi who would die.

"Darius!" called the voice of my master.

He had drawn the short straw, lost the roll of the dice, and our unit now had the unsavoury task of executing this man by crucifixion. A horrible death.

"Darius!" His voice sounded angrier, louder. "The drug… have you prepared it? Bring it now."

I had obeyed my orders and drugged the wine which would be served. I always obeyed orders. Well, almost always. In an act of rare defiance, today I had drawn many more drams of the costly myrrh than was necessary. I had taken hyssop, too, and added it to the wine they would give him—and it was a better wine than the vinegar-like ones typically used in crucifixions. If the Rabbi had to bear this horror, I'd make sure it was as painless as possible.

There would be consequences for my "mismeasurements," but in this moment my fear of punishment paled in the face of this opportunity to help my friend.

"Darius!" The centurion was now very angry with my tardiness.

I had to be brave, not a strong trait in my character, as I approached the cross. The wooden beam still lay on the ground. The crucifixion was only just beginning.

My heart and head swirled in turmoil. I had to calm myself. How had it come to this?

The Rabbi, my friend, lay prone on the horizontal cross, quiet and almost accepting of his fate. I remembered his words. He had described himself like a lamb brought to the slaughter…

I gulped.

Breathe, focus, I told myself. *That's the way to calm.*

He was bruised and bloodied. He had been whipped—from my training, I recognized the marks—and a hideous twine of brambles had been stuffed onto his head. I had seen much brutality in my life, but this? This was a vision I hoped never again to witness.

"Darius! Get on with it or you'll be the next one to go…"

My master's voice trailed off and I had to wonder whether he was upset with me. Or perhaps he was upset at himself. The centurion was hard to read.

I knelt beside the Rabbi.

"It's me, Darius, sir." I took the sleeve of my tunic, wiped away some of the dirt and blood from his face, and held the wine to his lips. "Please, Rabbi, drink this. It will help."

Calm, stay calm, I ordered myself. I always obeyed orders.

"It will help with the pain," I said. "I made it extra strong, to ease…"

His head turned away.

"Rabbi?" I prompted.

"Give it to the others, my friend." His voice always amazed me. I could always hear it, no matter where I was standing.

My friend? My head spun at his words. *How can he call me his friend? I'm helping his executioners!*

He turned toward me. "Go to the others. Help them."

I had been given an order and I always obeyed orders. I stood up and walked to the other two men nailed to their crosses.

"Darius!" My master was calling again. "The signs."

Officially, I was the centurion's scribe. That was one of the reasons I was here today. The other was to carry out my role in an unofficial capacity. I had been medically trained, after all.

I had been given the names of these convicted men and the crimes for which they were to be executed. I had to prepare the signs. The words would be written in three languages and nailed above each man's head prior to the lifting of the crosses. The scaffolding had already been erected.

I was a good scribe, proficient in many languages, so this was an easy task for me. However, in a moment of unusual bravery, I had somewhat altered the words I had been given for the Rabbi's sign. I had deliberately omitted a few crucial words: "He said he was." The sign now read:

Jesus the Nazarene: King of the Jews

There would be repercussions for this. Actions always had consequences. But at this moment, I didn't really care.

I handed the signs, neatly written, to my master. He read the first two, then paused at the third. He knew what I had done.

I couldn't read his face—again, he was a hard one to read—but I thought I may have seen a hint of a smile.

My reverie was interrupted by a disturbance. One of the soldiers had lifted his boot and struck a little dog that had ventured too close. It was Simi, who belonged to Little Simon.

I quickly intervened. "Pardon, sir, allow me to remove the beast," I said to the soldier using my very best slave-speak. "You have more pressing matters. Allow me."

He backed away while the dog crept forward and licked the Rabbi's face. As I watched this display, my thoughts turned to a story he had once told about dogs licking the face of a dying man...

I picked Simi up. "It's okay," I whispered.

I knew it wasn't, but I had to say something; the dog was shaking. I held him close, for comfort, but was it for the dog's or mine? I wasn't sure.

Simi just whimpered.

That's when I made a realization. Where was Big Simon? What about Simeon-of-the-knife? And the others, the Rabbi's many followers? Where were they?

I looked toward the crowd and spotted two women standing alongside each other, both named Mary. One was the Rabbi's mother. The other was from Magdala. Then I spotted another woman, his mother's sister, and young John. John was standing as close to the hill as the guards would allow.

Guilt smothered me. Had something I wrote caused this? I started to shake along with the little dog in my arms.

I had been instructed to remain on site until the end, as I was required to declare that the deaths had occurred. I'd also been told that Pilate had ordered that no bodies should remain on the crosses when the end came, something to do with the Sabbath. Jewish people had so many rules!

I needed to focus. Thinking helped. It muffled the sound of hammering, the screams…

I had trained myself from a very early age to avert my mind to avoid experiencing anything I dreaded. I needed to take my mind "away." When I did, my mentor all too often gave me a sharp cuff across the head and a stern order to focus. But being "away" kept me sane.

So I went "away," digging deep in my memory, determined to go to the beginning, to edit and analyze my responsibility for the events that had resulted in the Rabbi's execution…

PART ONE

Away

A
s I sat at the rear of the cart, looking back, I watched my familiar world—Fortress Antonia, the Temple Mount, the multi-storied limestone temple, the walls, and the gates of Jerusalem—fade into the distance. In that moment, I realized that I was now an itinerant scribe. I had been given a new assignment.

After several hours, the cart stopped. The driver who had been hired to transport me turned and spoke in Aramaic, telling me that we had arrived. I saw that he was pointing toward a small crowd that had gathered.

I thanked him in Aramaic, in proper slave position, and found myself standing alone in totally unfamiliar surroundings. How I wished that I were brave!

However, I had been given an order. So I approached the crowd but stood far to its edge, near a tree.

The man at the centre of this crowd was speaking of people and things with which I was unfamiliar. He spoke Aramaic with a northern accent; perhaps he was from Galilee. Had I passed this man on the street, I would have paid him no notice. He would have been just another Jew in from the country. But I couldn't help marveling at his voice: as far away as I was, his words sounded as clear as if I was standing right next to him.

I began copying his words, even though I knew not of those he was quoting. As a scribe, my job was to copy. I would transcribe the man's message from Aramaic to Latin later in the evening. I had been doing this for several weeks, following him unnoticed.

One late afternoon, having realized that I needed a flat surface for my parchments, I sat at a "table" I'd constructed from two rocks and a small board I'd carted along with me. I was completely unfamiliar with the nomadic lifestyle into which I'd been thrust. In fact, I knew nothing of any lifestyle that took me outdoors. I had no training except for a few simple instructions in how to start a fire. I'd also been given a bedroll, supplies for my writings, and coins to purchase food. I had exchanged my royal house tunics for more basic linens as well as a hooded robe to wear during frosty nights.

Gathering my thoughts, I wrote down the words that the Rabbi had spoken to those small crowds that always gathered to hear him speak. I had been given an order to report back on the man's activities and I always obeyed orders.

I was fluent in the local tongue and had to translate the Rabbi's words into Latin. An easy task for me.

Suddenly I was joined by a wiggly black puppy that jumped into my lap! It began to lick my face, a familiar sensation that I decided was not unpleasant. Who didn't like puppy kisses? I had held many such animals for Lucien. But I knew my face would be needing a good wash!

"Simi," called a child.

I looked up to see a young boy, perhaps six years old, running toward me.

He stopped abruptly and stared. At me? At the dog?

"Simi doesn't like strangers," the boy said. I could tell by the expression on his face that he was quite astonished. I was trained to read faces, and eyes in particular; eyes never lie.

I put the ball of fluffy dog down. "Perhaps, young master, you should share that information with Simi," I said politely. "He appears to have forgotten."

The boy laughed as the puppy began pawing at his toes in mock combat. The sight made me smile.

"I'm Little Simon," the boy replied. "Big Simon's my father. What's your name? You have yellow hair!"

"My name is Darius, young master. And you have black hair."

Again the child laughed. "What happened to your ear?"

My hand instinctively went to my notched right ear. "That, young master, marks me as born-slave. Should I ever be so foolish as to try to run away, that mark is how I would most certainly be identified."

"Does it hurt?" Concern appeared on Little Simon's face.

"No, young master, it doesn't hurt."

He approached and sat beside me—the dog, too. "What are you doing?"

"Well, young master, I'm writing down something the Rabbi said today. I change the words from your language into Latin, the one used by the Romans."

"You know how to do that?" His eyes studied me with suspicion.

"Yes, young master. It is an easy task."

"Why are you doing it?"

"I was ordered to do it, young master."

I always obey orders, I reminded myself.

"Do you know many tongues?" Little Simon asked.

So many questions. I had work to do, but I had to admit to myself that it was nice to have some company.

"Yes, young master, I do."

"Can you show me Simi's name in some of these other tongues?"

"Certainly, young master." I tore off a piece of parchment and wrote *Simi the dog* in ten different languages, explaining each one to the child.

"Little Simon!" called another voice.

The boy's head snapped up. "Oh, that's my mother. I have to go. Thank you. Bye."

With that, he ran toward the sound of his mother, all the while clutching the parchment as the puppy nipped at his heels.

I returned to the task at hand, but not for long. A group of men was approaching.

I was not brave, you see. It wasn't one of my assets. But I stood to face them, taking as respectful a posture as I could, trying to hide my fear.

"Who are you?" one of the men asked in an unfriendly tone. "What are you doing here?"

"I mean no disrespect, masters." I used my most humble slave-speak. "I am Darius, slave to centurion Marcus Longinus of the Third Imperial Legion. I was ordered to translate and transcribe the words of the one called the Rabbi and forward them. I'm only following orders, sirs."

I always follow orders, I wanted to add, but that would not have been appropriate.

"He's a Roman spy!" said a second man. This one was tall and imposing. "I should slit his throat right now."

I couldn't help but notice that this second man was in possession of a rather large knife. It hung from his belt in a sheath. I tried to remain calm, as I had been trained.

Breathe. Focus.

A third imposing figure stepped forward. "No one's cutting anyone's throat, Simeon."

I suddenly became aware that the first man was digging around in my bags, removing scrolls.

"He does possess the imperial seal," this man remarked, holding up the royal seal.

Please, I prayed to whatever god might be out there watching over slaves. *Please don't let the parchments be damaged. I have orders.*

"What's this?" demanded the one I internally named Simeon-of-the-knife.

"Indeed, sir, that is a royal seal," I said, trying to sound humble instead of terrified. My eyes and head were properly lowered. "Whenever I'm near a detachment, I am to take my transcripts, number each one, and seal them in the presence of the quartermaster, who in turn will forward them on… to my master, I assume. I don't know exactly. A mere slave isn't privy to such details. I am then allowed to restock my supplies and leave. I'm following orders."

"Best we take him to Jesus," said the one holding my bag and its many transcripts.

The man with the knife took charge. He pushed me and the group followed in line. We ascended the knoll in the same direction that the boy and his puppy had run toward a short while ago.

As we stopped just over the crest of the knoll, I saw a seated man, the same one whom I had been ordered to follow. The man with the voice. He appeared to be deep in thought as he sat waiting under a tree.

This man called Jesus, the Rabbi, looked up from what he had been doing, seeming more amused than surprised by my appearance before him.

"Welcome."

His voice wasn't unfriendly, but it unnerved me.

"Come, sit. Tell me about yourself and what you're doing so far from home." The Rabbi chuckled as he motioned for me to sit.

Again I tried to maintain my composure. Simeon-of-the-knife was standing close by my side. "Sir, it is not fitting for a mere slave to sit with a free man."

The Rabbi seemed quite amused by my discomfort and gestured. "Well then, sit over there."

Having been given an order, I moved further away. I sat. I always obeyed orders.

"You obviously aren't from around here," the Rabbi noted.

He was of course referring to my light-coloured hair, skin, shaved face, and tunic. I definitely was not Jewish.

"No sir, I'm not."

"What brings you here?" he asked.

"I am assigned as a scribe to centurion Marcus Longinus of the Third Legion out of Jerusalem. It is my order to transcribe your words—which I do, sir. Only your words. No interpretation on my part." I repeated the nature of my service. "I translate them into Latin, and then they are sent on to my master. I really don't know exactly who receives them, or where they go. I'm only the scribe. It's not my place to ask."

"He's also an idolator," Simeon-of-the-knife insisted, now handing the Rabbi a sketch that had been taken from my bag.

"I don't know or understand what that term means," I said, surprising myself by speaking before being spoken to. I had let my tongue outpace my brain.

But it was true. The term *idolator* left me befuddled.

The Rabbi didn't seem angry over my apparent lapse. "We don't condone what we call graven images—pictures, statues, or any symbol indicating worship to a false god. There is only one God, the great I Am, Yahweh."

"I meant no disrespect, Master." I knew it would do me no good for this group to consider me a blasphemer. "It can get quite lonely out here. Thus I often sketch a tree, a flower, a bird... not in adoration, you see. Rather in admiration of any Architect who could design such a thing." I let my mouth run, adding, "Didn't you once say that Yahweh sees value in even the sparrow?"

The Rabbi simply smiled.

Simeon-of-the-knife moved a little closer. A little too close, truth be told. I visualized his hands on my throat.

Thankfully, another one of the Rabbi's followers changed the direction of the conversation. "Teacher, I have read some of this man's writings. I have thought that we should be recording your instructions, for the future. It troubles me that there are so many deviations and misquotes of the Baptizer's preachings so soon after his death."

"Nonsense!" another spoke. "You so-called learned ones! We don't need your writings. We have the prophets' words inscribed in our memories, remembered in our temples and synagogues."

I feared that my presence among them had sparked discord.

"Friends, I'm sure our young guest could use some food and drink," the Rabbi interrupted. "I shall take him to the women while you continue your discussion. Come, Darius."

Since I always obeyed orders, I rose.

"I shall accompany you, Master," said Simeon-of-the-knife, my guard. "He is a stranger in our midst. Best we be cautious."

"As you wish, Simeon." The Rabbi looked amused.

The Rabbi led the way up a knoll to where a group of tents had been erected. Fires burned, children ran and played, and women sat chatting. But all these activities ceased as we approached.

"Darius... you came!"

I searched for the source of the young voice and found Little Simon hurrying toward me with his puppy.

"See, I told you," Little Simon called back to his friends. "He has yellow hair and a notch in his ear that doesn't hurt. He can also transcribe in lots of tongues."

The puppy, with its hackles raised, bared its teeth and ran toward my antagonist, a puppy-growl in its throat.

"You keep that cur away from me or I'll slit its mangy throat!" Simeon-of-the-knife shouted. He lifted a foot to give Simi a swift kick.

"Come, Simi," Little Simon called. "You stay away from Simeon or you'll get cooties!"

The other children roared in laughter as they ran off to continue their play.

I admired the child's courage. After all, I was not brave. Even the Rabbi chuckled.

We were soon joined by a captivating older woman whose tranquil demeanour unsettled me.

"Mother," the Rabbi said, embracing her. "This is Darius the scribe. I'm sure he'd enjoy some of tonight's stew."

"Welcome, Darius," the woman said with a smile.

The Rabbi gestured for me to sit, but I was reluctant.

"It is not proper..."

Simeon-of-the-knife grabbed my arm and forced me to sit.

I winced in pain.

"You're injured," the Rabbi remarked.

"It's nothing, sir. It's healing nicely." In my head, I added, *Or it was anyway.*

Simeon-of-the-knife pushed up my tunic sleeve to reveal the slave brand, still in the process of healing: it showed the mark of the royal house of Ceasar Augustus.

I had some explaining to do. "It is the mark of the emperor. I am the property of Caesar—"

"He's a spy!" Simeon-of-the-knife roared. "He must be killed, his body deeply buried and hidden, before the army of Rome descends upon us!"

The Rabbi remained calm. "Simeon, Simeon, let him complete his sentence."

"As a centurion's scribe, I was assigned to facilitate the paperwork," I said. "Forms, requisitions, troop assignments, merchants' orders for food, medical herbs… there are so many forms."

Calm down and breathe, the voice in my head reminded me.

"Now I've been ordered to transcribe your words, sir," I added. "The brand is a security measure. Should anyone take the seal, or should I lose it, it's indelible proof that I am an official scribe, thus entitled to supplies required for my duties. Who would brand himself for ink, parchment, and stylii?"

"Darius!"

I recognized this new voice. It belonged to Salome, a woman who worked as a cook in the palace kitchen.

"I knew it had to be you," Salome said as she arrived, standing next to the Rabbi's mother. "Not many have yellow hair! The kitchen girls will be so glad to hear you're still with us."

But for how long? I wondered to myself.

"Mary, Jesus… this young man is the delight of my kitchen staff. See? There it is… see how his face reddens?" She laughed heartily. Such a hearty laugh. "This may sound rather cheeky, but my staff and some of the laundry girls are in collusion. The laundry girls seem to only ever find *short* royal tunics for this one—so they can see him blush when they tease him about his knees. Very cheeky! Darius always takes it in stride."

I had always thought the girls did it on purpose! But now this seemed inconsequential. I said nothing.

"And he's as honest as they come," Salome continued. "Often the girls will carelessly over-order. Other scribes would fill the requisition, deliver the kitchen's needs, sell off the overage, and pocket the profit. Not Darius. He'd come back to the kitchen if he suspected an error. He'd correct the form. Darius has integrity."

My face reddened. Salome laughed.

Another woman now joined us. She had a most striking and beautiful face, which I couldn't help but notice as she placed a bowl in my hands. And to complicate matters, I later learned she was also a Mary, from the town of Magdala.

"You're hurt," the younger Mary remarked, eyeing the new scars I'd accumulated.

"It's nothing, mistress. It's healing nicely." I knew it was healing, but it was happening very slowly. I was a scribe now and had no access to medicine. I had been debriding the dead skin, but it would take time.

"Maybe. I'm not sure." Her voice sounded as pleasant as her face looked.

The younger Mary returned to the tent, soon to return with a jar of ointment. It was a local remedy; I didn't recognize the scent.

Gently, she applied a soothing layer of the ointment. I wasn't accustomed to the sensation of touch and tried to hold my arm still. The wound was still very sensitive, but her hands were as pleasant as her voice and face.

"He's a Gentile!" This from Simeon-of-the-knife again. "You're touching a Gentile and he's marked. Leviticus states—"

"He's injured!" Mary retorted. My presence was indeed a disruption to this community. "It should be treated again tonight and for the next few days."

If I'm still alive, I thought, but I kept my head and eyes in the proper lowered position.

"Thank you, mistress," I said.

The Rabbi turned to his mother. "Well, I shall leave our guest in your care and return to the men. When we're ready, let's have an evening campfire, all of us together—the men, women, and children. I'll send John when it's time."

He gave his mother a warm embrace. There was something about her; even with my extensive vocabulary, I couldn't retrieve the correct word…

"Eat, Darius." And with that, the Rabbi left. It was as if he knew: I always obeyed orders.

Simeon-of-the-knife remained close by my side, however.

The women chatted. Children played. A puppy barked. A woman sang to a child in her arms. I knew little of such connections. I felt fearful, and now unsettled. I kept my eyes lowered, which was the correct thing to do. After all, these were all freeborn.

The one called John appeared, calling the women, children, Simeon-of-the-knife, and myself to join the Rabbi around the fire.

Simeon-of-the-knife grabbed my arm and pushed me down.

"Darius, tell us about yourself," the Rabbi said in a kind voice.

"Myself?" I was confused. "Sir, I am slaveborn. My story is nothing."

"My young friend, no person's story is *nothing*. You have experienced much and seen places none of us could even imagine. We will all benefit from learning about your past, where you've been and what you've witnessed. All of this makes you *you*. I spend my entire day talking. It would please me for another orator to take over." The Rabbi smiled. "That's an order."

"Speak," Simeon-of-the-knife demanded.

I didn't know what to say. I'd never encountered such a command.

"Where do you come from?" The question came from Little Simon's mother.

"Why's your hair that color?" asked a child's voice, eliciting smiles and chuckles.

Even I smiled.

Breathe, calm, focus, I thought, looking up.

"I come from far away," I began. "From Tuscany, a hilly area where it's always green and lush and the air is always fresh. Very different from Israel. The countryside is dotted with manors, fine homes, the summer residences of wealthy merchants and Rome's elite. Rome is hot and the air is heavy in summer. That's where I was born. Well, not at a manor but rather a ludus, part of a very large estate. The master was very wealthy. The place, known as a ludus, was a training facility for future gladiators and overseen by one simply known as the Dom, a gladiator who had won many victories. He was a powerful, formidable force but still a capable and fair instructor. His trainees were well-fed, well-housed, well-trained, and well-tended when injured.

"That's where I was birthed anyway. I assume that my hair and skin colouring arose from those who caused me to be. I have no memory of any father or mother. I have difficulty relating to the concept. You see, babies birthed at the facility were a commodity, to be sold to local estates or at the markets in Rome. This was all part of the master's business. The young were raised as a cohort in a nursery. All their basic needs were met, making a mother unnecessary."

"Don't you miss your mother?" asked a young girl with wide eyes.

"Young mistress, no. I never had a mother."

"That is *so* wrong!" This came from another girl, one whom I had heard being called Olivia. She sounded forceful and very angry. "How could you not miss your mother?"

She hugged the one I assumed must be her mother but continued to glare at me.

I didn't want these people to think I was a monster, so I entered into dialogue with young Olivia. I suddenly realized I had never interacted with a child before—with the exception of the chance encounter I'd had with Little Simon and his dog just a few hours past. I was fluent in many tongues and dialects, but I had no training in child-speak.

"Young mistress..." I tried to make my voice gentle, as when soothing a startled horse. Of this, I had some experience. "You indeed would miss your mother if you were to be separated from her. And I assume she, your mother, would experience the same emotion. You two are bonded."

Bonded? I wondered whether that term was appropriate.

Olivia continued to glare, so I had to try harder. If my presence were to cause nightmares in these children's dreams, the parents might line up behind Simeon-of-the-knife. I had to continue, had to make her understand.

"Logically, young mistress, I cannot miss what I never had."

Logically? What does a child know of logic? My brain was talking now. *Give the child a concrete example.*

The boy and the dog!

"Take Simi," I added. "He is newly weaned, but even so he is ready, young as he is, to protect Little Simon."

The rest of the camp had witnessed the recent encounter of Simi with Simeon-of-the-knife.

I continued. "Simi and his young master are bonded. They know each other But, what if a merchant from far away had taken Simi from his littermates before he knew the young master? Imagine that the merchant took Simi across the desert to Egypt as a gift for his son. Would

Simi miss his young master? Would the young master miss Simi? No. They would have no connection. You cannot miss what you do not have."

The girl was a formidable opponent, however, and seemed determined not to give up. Instead she offered a new and clever twist.

"You are standing here," Olivia insisted. "You therefore have a mother—and a father. The law of Moses states that one must honour both."

Her words were like a blow to the chest. She had bested me! Outmanoeuvred me. It was brilliant, I had to admit it. We were in Jewish territory, on her turf, and my life was at stake here, not hers.

In my head, I recalled the words of an old instructor: *"At the point of having been outplayed, when you realize that pressing on may end badly, it is best to defer to your opponent."*

"Young mistress, you have given me much to think on," I said. "Thank you for giving me these insights. Thank you for enlightening me."

My brain chided me. *You spent five years at one of the finest seats of academia—and here you are, bested by a child!*

Olivia's mother spoke. "I apologize for my daughter's boldness, for interrupting. She can be quite outspoken."

She's brilliant, I wanted to say. Instead I silenced the words before they could come out.

"Continue, please," said the Rabbi, who seemed to be amused by all this.

I continued, trying hard not to sound ruffled by what had just transpired. "Where I grew up, the other boys my age would playfight with sticks, imitating the actions of the trainees. My interest in the gladiators was entirely different. They came from all over the empire and spoke so many tongues… I was fascinated by the variety of tongues, particularly upon first arrival. The sounds—some harsh, some guttural, some lilting—were like music, captivating me.

"Lucien, the physician, noticed me. He asked permission to take me as his protégé, as young as I was. I would learn his skills over time, but for now I was big enough to carry his bag and fetch vials and herbs. These chores I did efficiently. I was encouraged to learn the tongues, the languages, as it would make diagnosis easier if I could communicate.

"I was like a sponge, according to Lucien, and that became my nickname. He too was a slave. I knew not whether he was slaveborn or freeborn, or where he came from; it was not my place to inquire. But he was a most skilled physician. He not only treated the trainees but was also sent to the other manors to treat both humans and animals. 'A body is a body,' he would say. 'Man, woman, young, old, human, animal… they're like machinery, with all the same working parts.' Often he'd awaken me from sleep, saying, 'Wake up, Sponge, or I'll wring you out.'"

The children who were still awake, for it was late in the evening now, giggled at this.

They must not look upon me as a monster, I reminded myself.

"I was called to the manor house when I was perhaps a mid-teen," I continued. "I was to accompany the young master as his house-slave to a place called Alexandria. Lucien explained to me that I'd be visiting the seat of knowledge, a capital city where there was an excellent academy.

"But I soon learned my real role. The young master wasn't interested in academia. He knew of my linguistic facility, though, and meant for me to attend his classes, write his essays, and take his exams. He wanted no part of school. He wanted no part of me, in fact. He arranged for a small room near the school and provided me a stipend to cover the basics. The situation suited us both. The tutors must have known of the arrangement. It was so obvious. But I was never called out.

"I spent the next five years there. I had so much to learn. After those five years, with my dissertations complete, I awaited the results. Soon I was summoned to the faculty building, one which no student could enter except to be dismissed for poor grades or improper behaviour. And I had been summoned!

"Fortunately, I had made a friend during my years in Alexandria. Balzak was socially and physically my opposite, but I considered him to be like a brother. He insisted on accompanying me to the door of the faculty building. I'm not brave, you see. Thus my friend's insistence that he accompany me, for I feared being sent home in shame. I was, after all, a fraud.

"I recognized most of the assembled panel of instructors. I was told to sit and I complied. The head instructor then stated that many previous students had tried to substitute a ringer—and they knew I was just such a one. After all, I hardly looked Roman. One of my instructors spoke next, explaining that my name had come up after the first term when the faculty was culling the number of students. They of course realized that I wasn't who I claimed to be, but my scores were so outstanding for someone in my position that I had obviously been well-started in life.

"Everyone agreed to allow me to continue, to see what my brain was capable of achieving. I became their experiment. The head instructor had thought I should be made aware of their ruse, however. Although the certificate would be issued in my master's name, I was the one who had passed all the classes. Even with a heavy course load, I was head of the class.

"The young master and I returned to Rome. Officially he was fully matriculated—head of the class, to the delight of his father. And I was returned to Tuscany.

"Eventually, the young master assumed his father's position upon the latter's death and I was summoned back to Rome to run the affairs of his business. Summer was nearing, and the air was hot and heavy. Rome boils in summer, so we returned to Tuscany. During this time, my master entertained a host of guests and I was given the extra duty of arranging food and entertainment for his banquets.

"It also turned out that he had a favourite companion, and she wanted to see a battle to the death. I protested. Such had never before been allowed, since this was strictly a training ground. I let my mouth run away from my brain and defied him. I spoke above my station.

"There are consequences for such outbursts and my master ordered me flogged, but not to death. Lucien intervened and convinced the master I was still of some value.

"What happened next, though, was all my fault. I should have employed tact, handled the situation differently. During a contest, at the point in combat when the victor was to make the final kill, he instead hurled his weapon into the loge, striking the master and killing him. A riot ensued! So many were killed, Lucien among them.

"Afterward I woke up recovering in the infirmary. I was safe. But because the master had died without an heir, the entire manor became the property of Ceasar Augustus—so, yes, I am indeed the property of the emperor now.

"At first my duties were of a minor capacity in Rome. Then I was sent to Jerusalem and assigned to serve as a scribe under centurion Marcus Longinus, perhaps because I am fluent in your language and its dialects, both in its spoken and written forms.

"And then I was given the order to follow you and report on your sayings. First I had to be marked. I should have been given the brand of the royal house earlier, but it hadn't been done. After all, the royal seal alone isn't enough. It could be lost or stolen. When I take my transcripts to a detachment, the quartermaster must require them to be waxed and sealed. He would need to see my brand as indelible proof of my authenticity…"

I trailed off, my long story drawing to an end. What more could I say? But I felt there was a bit more.

"Sir, I meant only to follow orders, not to intrude or cause discord among your followers. If I am a spy, it should be apparent that I've failed. I never interpreted my mission here to be one of spying. I'm just recording, summarizing, and submitting. But I do understand how my actions could be considered espionage. I have not considered all the ramifications. It is not my place to question, but to obey my master."

But I do know the consequences of defying an order, I told myself.

The Rabbi turned and gestured to one of his followers who I remembered from earlier. "Matthew is correct," he said. "My words will be recorded. Future generations will read them. Matthew, have you read this man's transcripts? Are they accurate?"

The one named Matthew nodded. "They are, Teacher. He has a facility for recording what has been spoken without offering interpretation. He is very well educated for a… for his position. I would be interested in reading his reports to confirm their accuracy and jog my own memory before they are turned over to the Romans. His reports are good. I admire his style."

I felt my face redden.

"Darius," the Rabbi said, looking me in the eye. "Have you been forbidden to share what you write before the documents are sealed?"

"No, sir. No such ban has ever been issued."

Another spoke. "If these reports failed to appear, would it not draw the attention of Rome?"

A man who was dressed much more finely than the others leaned forward. "Let the legions come, I say. It's time to rise up and rid our nation of the yoke of Caesar!"

"Really, Judas, what are you going to do?" yet another man asked. "Blow a trumpet and watch the Romans tumble down?"

This response drew a round of laughter.

"Listen to me," Judas continued. "Simeon has access to the manpower; I, the resources. We know people. We have connections. Arms can be purchased, men trained—"

"Have you forgotten what happened to Judas of Gamala?" another follower angrily broke in. "He thought likewise. And what did he accomplish? Have you also forgotten Sepphoris? Such grandiose ideas lead to crucifixion, not the end of Roman occupation!"

Many of the men and women nodded, expressing their agreement.

All this talk of rebellion startled me. I would not report any of this, of course. My order was to record only what the Rabbi preached.

When I looked over to him, I realized that the Rabbi had lowered his head, preventing me from reading his eyes. He was scratching lines in the sand with a twig. I could not read his eyes.

"The Rabbi has never advocated any form of violence or insurrection," a woman said in the ensuing silence. Her voice was soft yet emphatic. "His message focuses on salvation, not liberation from Rome. He speaks of the path that leads to Yahweh."

I saw the Rabbi smile.

"My mother is right," said another man. "Let the scribe report. We have nothing to hide. The Rabbi's words should be noted. Gentiles, even soldiers, are often present in the crowds and the Rabbi doesn't order them away. We have nothing to hide."

Another man I didn't know replied, "You realize that we are talking insurrection in front of an agent of Tiberius."

All eyes turned to me. I felt their intensity! My presence was indeed causing some upheaval amongst the Rabbi's followers and I felt afraid. I was not brave.

Breathe, calm, focus…

"Apologies, sirs, for speaking before being given permission to do so," I ventured. "But I am not Roman, hence I cannot be an agent of the emperor. I owe no allegiance or loyalty to Caesar. I am a mere slave, given an order pertaining only to the one known as the Nazarene. I only follow that order. What others say or do is none of my concern."

The Rabbi spoke directly to me. "I don't believe you're a spy. You were obeying an order—I sense that you always obey orders, which you may continue to do." He raised his hand before Simeon-of-the-knife could object. "You may stay or you may go, scribe. The decision is yours. Life is all about making decisions. My Father extends to humans the gift of free choice. But I must insist that you move closer to the fire at night. For one with such a brain, it's a wonder the hyenas haven't devoured you."

I stayed that night, and I did move closer to the fire, but I remained on the periphery, with my guard keeping a close eye on me.

Two women returned later that night, the beautiful Mary Magdelene and Salome. Mary brought more ointment and Salome carried a blanket. Neither of them would hear any of my protests.

"Romans, they know nothing of desert nights," said Salome. "Their blankets, totally useless."

"My lady, may I ask a question?"

"Of course, Darius."

"What is a hyena?"

I slept well that night. Simeon-of-the-knife remained by my side; somehow it helped me to feel safe.

I rose early the next morning, before dawn, to find the camp asleep. I got up to perform my morning ablutions, recalling that Lucien had always been fastidious about hygiene. I was obsessive about it too. I needed to clean away all the blood and putrid bandages… I couldn't bear even a stain on my tunic; where had that spot come from?

While returning to my spot, I hoped that my guard hadn't yet awakened and alerted the others to catch me before I could warn the nearest Roman garrison.

"Darius," called the Rabbi. He was sitting on a knoll, facing east where the sun was just barely showing itself. "Come, sit. I order it."

He was smiling. He knew I couldn't disobey.

"The journey won't always be an easy one," he remarked.

I didn't quite understand where this was leading. "The journey, sir?"

"Life is a journey, for each of us. The terminus leads to the face of Yahweh." The man's face was beginning to reflect the sunrise. "Look, soon it will be dawn. This nation will join as one, all facing east. We praise God each morning thus."

"I'm sure He is well pleased." I hesitated, though, for I had spoken out of turn. "I apologize, Master. Sometimes my mouth proceeds my brain. And I'm sorry that I have sown discord in your group. Perhaps it's best if I leave."

Leave and face the consequences, I added to myself. *Rome doesn't look kindly upon failure.*

"There is friction," he acknowledged. "A Gentile, and a slaveborn one at that, discovered recording my words? Of course there would be cause for concern. My followers come from diverse backgrounds, from humble to affluent, literate to illiterate, a tax-collecting cheat to those who are nearly saints. They are just beginning this journey, works in progress, each trying to find their place. They will, in time, become a cohesive unit and change the world. But not yet. They have much to learn." He turned to look at me, studying me closely. "Darius, you have a choice to make. Everything comes down to choice. And as you well know, actions have consequences."

He stood up.

"Now I must return. It's almost sunrise."

I continued to obey the order I'd been given to report on the Rabbi. I witnessed miraculous occurrences beyond the capabilities of the most skilled of physicians: blind eyes sighted, deaf ears opened, the lame and crippled restored to full mobility… yet never once did the Rabbi ask for, or take, a cash reward. "Tell no one," he often advised.

As for his message, clearly there was nothing in it to alarm Rome. He never spoke of insurrection, rebellion, or civil disobedience. He advised that masters be good masters, that slaves be good slaves, that soldiers act with fairness, that tax collectors take only what was owed.

No, there was nothing in it to raise Rome's alarm, even though the area around Jerusalem was known to be a hotbed of turmoil.

In one particularly remarkable incident, a huge crowd had gathered to see the Rabbi, for he had developed a reputation as a healer. A well-dressed and obviously well-placed gentleman approached through the crowd that day and everyone parted in deference to one of such importance. He asked, even begged the Rabbi to come. His only child, a young daughter, was dying from a wasting disease. There was no cure.

While on his way, accompanying the distraught man, the Rabbi had stopped and demanded to know who had touched his robe. That was curious, for the crowd was so large. And yet the Rabbi said that he felt a trickle of power leave his body.

A middle-aged woman fell at his feet. Even from a distance, I could make the diagnosis: blood loss. The woman was anaemic, and a rather severe case.

She begged for the Rabbi's forgiveness, as she'd meant him no harm. She had hoped that just by touching his garment, not interrupting him, she might regain her strength.

The Rabbi said nothing. He just smiled at her and moved on.

I had an order—to follow the Rabbi and report. And I always obeyed. Almost always. For I could not leave this woman alone in the street after the crowd had moved on.

I explained to her that I was connected with the Rabbi and had some medical training. She seemed not to care that I was so obviously a Gentile, let alone a slave, and thanked me for my offer of assistance.

Once I had supported her and we began to walk, she told me that she could feel her strength returning.

I diagnosed her as suffering from hysteria. But her colour was returning. Her lips were no longer blue and I discreetly felt for a pulse; it was strong and steady. The eyes never lied, and in her case they were alert and responsive. She was indeed in recovery.

So many social boundaries had already been broken since my arrival in this area, and I didn't wish to cause more. So I left her at her doorway and continued on to locate the house where the Rabbi had gone.

When I arrived there, I came upon a large crowd. Apparently the child had already died and the paid mourners, part of the cultural death protocol, were waiting. I assumed that the Rabbi was inside, offering solace to the parents.

Had I been within, I would have checked the girl to confirm that death had occurred. Lucien had taught me to recognize the signs.

At last the Rabbi and the parents emerged, but the latter were hardly grieving. Hysteria, I again diagnosed.

"She lives!" the father proclaimed. "The Rabbi told her to wake up… she lives!"

In shock, I decided that I would have to report this. But of course I would add, for the first time, the comment that I hadn't come into contact with the body to verify her death.

News of such magnitude could not be contained. The size of the crowds grew.

I conceded that Rome might be concerned about the Rabbi's popularity. He was known as a teacher, and I reported this fact accurately. He was preaching only the age-old message of the Golden Rule, a message I had dissected many times in my philosophy tutorials. And I never forgot the Rabbi's reminder that actions do have consequences.

The Rabbi's voice always amazed me. No matter where one stood in a crowd, it was always audible. It sounded like music. His stories, parables designed for the adult ear, were engaging, driving home lessons that rural folk could understand. He related his messages to seeds and planting, weeds and reaping, even errant sons. Aesop would have been proud.

Rabbi was in the middle of telling a lesson about a good shepherd finding a lost lamb when I became aware of the sensation of warm breath on my neck.

The centurion's horse!

I turned in surprise and found myself looking up at my master, Marcus Longinus, who beckoned for me to follow him away.

I had no choice. I obeyed orders, almost always.

As we walked away from the gathering, I held the horse's bridle.

The centurion didn't dismount. "You know this man, the Rabbi?"

Of course! It's your order I'm following... but I silenced my mouth before any words came out.

"Yes, master." I took the proper position, my head and eyes lowered.

"Is there any trickery in the feats he is said to perform?" The centurion's voice was unfriendly and cold-edged.

I assumed he was referring to the stories now circulating about his miraculous cures. I had to answer carefully.

"Trickery—?"

He cut me off. "None of your slave-speak. You can be so annoying! Are the stories real or not?" He was angry! "Are you even capable..."

The horse, sensing its rider's agitation, began to prance. I was not a horse-keeper of any sort, but I had some training. I stroked the beast's neck.

"Sir, he asks for no money and helps everyone, from the poorest to the wealthiest," I explained. "I have some training, and I have seen no deceit. In my humble opinion, there is no trickery."

"Get me an audience with him. Now."

"Now, sir?"

Don't you see the crowd? I wanted to ask. *How am I to do this now?*

I knew the Rabbi always had the crowd rest and eat toward the day's hottest hour, so I looked to the sky. Indeed, it was nearing that time of day.

Again, my master bellowed at me. "Now!"

I prayed to whatever slave-helping god might be available that the centurion and the horse would remain right where they were. I feared alarming the likes of Simeon-of-the-knife, since he still frightened me. I was not brave.

I made my way through the crowd.

"Rabbi?" I called out as I approached.

"Yes, Darius, can I help you?" Although the Rabbi spoke the question, I suspected he already knew about the request that was to come.

"My master, the centurion… he's here," I said. "He requests an audience. It seems to be of an important nature." I tried to sound both humble and stress the urgency of the situation. I preferred the written word.

Simeon-of-the-knife had overheard the conversation; either that or he had seen the horse and rider at the edge of the gathering. The horse, after all, was a rather tall animal.

"He's brought the legion!" Simeon said to the Rabbi. "I told you this would end badly!"

The Rabbi smiled. "You're exaggerating. This is but one Roman soldier." He hesitated for a moment. "But you're right… this will end badly. Just not right now. Yes, Darius, tell the centurion to approach. Of course I'll speak with your master."

Simeon-of-the-knife, my antagonist, threw up his hands as I left to deliver the message.

I returned to the centurion, told him the Rabbi's words, and then followed as he led the way back to where Jesus was waiting. The crowd parted for us, more likely out of fear than respect.

Before long, we faced the Rabbi.

Please, I prayed to whatever slave-helping god might be available. *Make the centurion get off his horse…*

I held the horse as my master thankfully dismounted. I made the introductions, after which the two men walked away.

As they conversed, Simeon waited at my side. From the look of daggers he kept throwing my way, I could imagine him pressing his knife to my throat.

After only a few moments, the centurion and the Rabbi returned to where I was holding the reins of my master's horse. I couldn't read the centurion's face as he mounted. He was a hard one to read.

Before turning to go, though, he faced the Rabbi and gave him the centurion's salute, an honour usually only bestowed on those highly placed.

As suddenly as he came, my master was gone.

"A kind man, your master, so concerned over the health of one employed in his house," the Rabbi said. "A kind man."

The centurion is efficient, I thought, *but hardly kind.*

We travelled throughout the country, and into Samaria too. Always the Rabbi's message was the same: the good news he spoke of would bring peace to those who shared and showed compassion to the weak, the stranger, and even the enemy. He spoke of a final judgment when a proverbial shepherd would separate the goats from the sheep—goats to the slaughter, sheep to lie in lush green pastures. Actions would have consequences, he warned.

As we were walking one day through the countryside, we saw some figures approaching us from the distance. We heard shouts as we got nearer.

"Unclean!"

The prospect of contagion has always terrified me. I was not brave. Hence my obsession with cleanliness. I was always on the lookout for blood, stained bandages, and open sores.

"Unclean! Unclean!"

The group froze, but not the Rabbi. He continued forward until he had walked right up to them. To my astonishment, he even touched them! Touched their disease-riddled bodies!

Bathing in the water of a dozen seas still wouldn't be enough to cleanse these poor souls of their flesh-destroying illness. It was incurable.

And yet the Rabbi stepped right into their midst.

Jubilant shouts rang out as these lepers tossed aside their bandages. The physician in me felt curiosity pushing me on. I just had to quell my revulsion.

I inched nearer, wondering what had happened. Was it possible the Rabbi had healed them? Several of the men and women out front certainly appeared to have patches of clear, healthy skin.

The Rabbi, with the touch of his hand and his eyes raised to his God, seemed to have done what even the most skilled physician could not; he had cured leprosy!

The Rabbi asked for no reward. Instead he sent them on their way, according to their law, to present themselves to a rabbi before re-entering society.

Only one came back to thank him, and I sensed that this disappointed the Rabbi. I read it in his eyes. Eyes never lie. Ten had been cured, but only one offered thanks.

At times groups of women and children joined us for a while before returning home. But during the rainy season, everyone left us to return to their villages. Even I would return to Jerusalem and my duties there.

But there came a time when our group disbanded, and it wasn't the rainy season.

The Rabbi decided to send his disciples—that's the word he now used to describe his closest followers—out in pairs to do what he had been doing—teaching and healing in the name of his Father, Yahweh, the great I Am. They were not to take money along, nor were they to accept any. I admired their courage.

In the meantime, the Rabbi intended to return to Capernaum, by the Sea of Galilee, where his mother Mary lived. He thought of Capernaum as home.

"Come, Darius," the Rabbi told me on the day of his departure. "You can be of some service."

His words confused me, but he had ordered me to follow him—and of course I always obeyed orders.

In Capernaum, I learned of a different version of this man. The Rabbi was a teacher, a healer, and also a carpenter. He had learned this trade from a man he fondly referred to as Joseph, the husband of his mother Mary. Joseph was now long dead.

I learned that the Rabbi had some carpentry orders to catch up on. I knew nothing of woodworking, so I joined him in the shop to watch, handing him the tools he required. After all, a saw was a saw.

He rarely accepted payment even in this capacity, whether for rehanging a sagging door or refashioning an ox yoke to fit a new beast. He'd just smile and say "Next time, when the crops are in."

I never actually entered the house in Capernaum, since I was both slaveborn and a Gentile. My presence at his side was already a source of gossip.

Instead I kept myself isolated, sitting and musing—I went "away," as I often did, out in the courtyard.

One day the Rabbi went out to measure a local rabbi's house for shelving, leaving me to tarry in the yard of his mother's house.

Suddenly, she was beside me! Mary, his mother. Her presence always unnerved me.

I prepared to rise, the proper code of conduct when approached by a freeborn, but she was too quick. I had been "away", daydreaming.

She settled herself on the bench beside me. I felt trapped.

"Darius," Mary said in a soft voice. She was always soothing. "We need to talk please."

What could I do? Where could I go?

"Yes, my lady, do you require something?" I tried to sound matter-of-fact.

"I need to know why you fear me."

"Fear you, my lady?" Where was this conversation going?

"Please speak openly. Have I offended you somehow?"

She had asked a question and I had to respond. I always had to obey. I swallowed hard. *Breathe, calm, focus.*

"No, my lady, you have never offended me," I said. "It's just that…"

"Continue. It's okay. You are allowed to converse with what you call a freeborn, and a Jew, and a woman. It's okay, please. I really want you to continue."

She'd given me another order.

"You… you unnerve me." There, I'd said it aloud.

"Continue, please," she replied in that unsettling voice. "Please explain why I *unnerve* you."

Breathe, calm, focus.

"I sense, my lady, that not only is your son..." I struggled for the correct terminology. "...otherborn—hence, his remarkable abilities—but you too are not slaveborn, or freeborn... I think you too are otherborn..." I took another breath before continuing. "I know it's illogical, but you unnerve me. I mean you no disrespect."

She smiled. "None taken. I do have a mother, a father, siblings, relatives... I am *normal*."

"Begging to differ, my lady, but I sense you are in no way normal. That is what unnerves me. My brain has... difficulty... with you. I have a very logical brain."

She still smiled. "Something did happen to me many years ago. I was very young, a teen. It could have led to my death. In that, we have something in common. We've both found our lives in peril. Joseph saved me. He found wisdom and married me knowing that Jesus, the child growing within me, was not his." She looked wistful. I knew the look; she was "away." "Joseph... he was such a good person. I miss him. Every day, I miss him."

She averted her gaze, consumed by a wave of emotion.

"We also share another connection, Darius," she added. "We both bear guilt. We carry it within us. Others have died because of us."

I found her words to be confusing.

"Soon after my son's birth, soldiers came. Babies were slaughtered... I'm still haunted by the mothers' screams... I bear their grief." She shuddered. "Yes, we both share guilt. But you look confused, and rightly so. My son's birth was normal—in the human sense. We were in Bethlehem, to be counted in Augustus's great census and pay taxes. Let me retrace, though. Are you familiar with the term 'angel'?"

Mary was asking a question and I had to respond. I always obeyed orders.

"Yes, my lady. Disembodied spirits from either the upperworld or underworld. Some act as guardians. Others wreak havoc and bring chaos. The existence of such beings has been often discussed. But it was long ago."

"We believe they exist," Mary said. "Many of our prophets reported seeing them, then discoursing with them, even eating with them. I saw an angel. I was alone in my house and everyone was out. I was at my loom. Like you, I daydream. My mind was 'away.' Joseph was in Egypt with his kinfolk, also skilled tradesmen, working on a big project. He'd be gone for months. I was planning my house, furniture, the wedding... like I said, I was 'away.'

"Then there was a voice. I startled. A figure appeared... and he said his name was Gabriel, an archangel, a messenger for the great I Am, Yahweh. Of course I was terrified—like you, I find it difficult to be brave.

"Our people have long awaited the coming of a Messiah, the one to make all the wrongs committed by mankind right with God. It would be a human act of redemption. A prophecy stated that a virgin shall bring forth a child, the Messiah. And Gabriel was asking me to be the mother of this child..."

Mary stopped and fixed her gaze on me.

"Yes, I can see your confusion," she said. "Shall I stop? Do you need time...?"

"No, my lady, I'm fine." I wasn't. "Please continue."

"I could have... *should* have been stoned. An unwed mother, with child? I was visibly pregnant by the time Joseph arrived home. But he too was visited by Gabriel. He too saw the angel. He understood. And so we were married and came to Bethlehem to be counted in the great census. It was time. I assure you, his birth was indeed human!

"Shepherds from the hillside also saw and heard angels. The Messiah had arrived, and they knew where to find us. The town was crowded, so we'd found shelter in an inn's stable. It was clean and warm and there were animals. I love animals. I had Joseph. I had my son. And now I had visitors. The shepherds brought us useful, thoughtful gifts—cheeses, broths, bread, and yogurt.

"Other visitors came—the Magi, astronomers from away. They'd been following a new star. There had been another ancient prophecy about a new star appearing in the sky heralding the birth of a new king." She paused for a moment. "You studied astronomy. Did you learn of such a star?"

"Yes, my lady. The star's appearance was reported. Its significance was much debated."

I could understand this part of her story. It was logical.

"The Magi brought far more valuable gifts. These helped us when we relocated, for the current King Herod's father, also a Herod, had heard that the star marked the birth of a baby king. Believing only his lineage could hold title, he sent troops and ordered them to kill all the boys two years old and under living in or around Bethlehem. And soldiers, like you, always obey orders.

"We escaped. Later Joseph had another visit from Gabriel, who told us we were to flee to Egypt. We listened to the angel's warning and were spared. I still have the guilt, though. So many innocents are dead. Darius, we have much in common—our reveries, our guilt… but honestly, I am human. Please don't be unnerved by me. I'm not otherborn."

Mary smiled and patted my hand. It was not unpleasant.

Afterward she rose and left—and I was still unnerved.

There was a second astounding event in Capernaum—this one not so unnerving. But unexpected? Definitely.

The Rabbi and I had delivered the bookcase he had been contracted to build. He was skilled and it was an impressive piece. I, of course, remained outside the house when we arrived.

"Darius, you're alive!"

I turned at the sound of this long-forgotten voice, shocked to see my friend Balzack, a fellow student I had gotten to know in Alexandria. I befriended him despite Lucien's warnings.

"I thought you were dead," Balzack said, looking amazed to see me. He was tall, black, elegantly dressed, and perhaps a little heavier than I remembered.

"Wrong again!" I smiled. "What are you doing—?"

I couldn't finish because his immense arms suddenly closed around me and lifted me off the ground.

By now the Rabbi had emerged from the house and I made the introductions. I looked around, worried about us being seen. There would be gossip, I feared, with the Rabbi walking with two Gentiles, one blond and short and the other quite the opposite.

The three of us settled in the house's courtyard. The Marys, both the Rabbi's mother and the young one I found so beautiful, brought refreshments and sat with us. More social conventions smashed, I feared. But no one other than myself seemed to care.

"Darius saved my life," Balzack recalled. "I was so lonely and homesick in Alexandria. It was hard to be so far from my homeland and I found the classes difficult. So I decided to end my life. I stood on the ledge of one of the academy's taller structures, thinking I was alone. But it turns out I wasn't." He grinned at me. "I know what you're thinking, Darius. 'Wrong again.' I looked over and saw you, a pale-skinned, blond-haired fellow freshman, standing at my side. I remember your words: 'Pardon, master. I too often stand here absorbing the view, marvelling at the expanse of the cosmos and the earth's relationship to the universe. Are you looking toward your homeland? It must be a comfort to know someone is awaiting your return.' You talked me down. You never questioned me. Never judged. You just invited me to share in your meagre meal. Turns out it was the best I'd ever dined on. You saved me from the abyss.

"I tried to find you later because I wanted to buy your freedom. I would offer the option for you to come and join me in running the family business. So I went to Tuscany, and when I got there I was told that there had been an insurrection. Everyone was killed. That's why I thought you were dead. But I named my next son after you. Young Darius doesn't look a bit like you!"

I noticed that others had entered the courtyard, among them Little Simon. His eyes were huge as he saw Balzack for the first time.

"Oh, the escapades we had!" my friend crowed, nudging me.

My face reddened and I prayed again, to whatever slave-helping god was out there, to please silence him.

Balzack laughed and said no more.

Thank you, god, wherever you are.

But the silence didn't last for long.

"With the help of Darius and that brain of his, I did graduate and make my family proud," Balzack added. "Despite our physical differences, I'm proud to call him a brother." I couldn't help but notice that he failed to mention our obvious social differences. "But seriously, Darius, who is your current master? I'll offer a queen's ransom to purchase you and obtain your freedom."

His eyes revealed that he was serious.

"I'm afraid it would take a king's ransom." I raised my tunic sleeve to reveal the emperor's brand. "Wrong again."

Balzack went on to explain that he was in Capernaum to await a caravan. He had been in the area for business for some time now and would be leaving the following day.

With another off-the-ground hug and a farewell, I felt Balzack slip something into my hand. I looked down at the large pearl. Perhaps it was a gem of much value, which the Rabbi had once spoken of.

I felt honoured, but I immediately removed the gem and handed it back. "Thank you, brother, but I cannot accept this."

"Why not?" Balzack was dumbfounded.

"Possessing an object of such value would put me in great danger. It would be assumed I had stolen it. No slave could legally possess such a treasure."

"I hadn't thought of that."

"Never your strong point, thinking," I pointed out, employing some levity. Lucien had often suggested developing my sense of humour. "Give it to my namesake, brother. Perhaps he'll attend the academy someday."

"Consider it done."

And with that, and another of his hugs, Balzack was gone. I knew that I'd never see him again, not in this lifetime.

Little Simon and Simi ran up to me.

"He's so big," the boy said admiringly. "But I wasn't really scared. I knew Simi would protect me."

I marvelled at the open honesty of this child. No wonder the Rabbi often encouraged adults to be like little children.

"You know, young master," I said, preparing to quote my teacher's words, "no matter male or female, young or old, human or animal, a body is a body."

We continued on in silence. I hoped I had given the young master some insight.

The disciples began returning to Capernaum from their individual missions, two by two. They were full of stories of their adventures spreading the Rabbi's "good news", as he called it, and healing in his Father's name. Apparently they too had obeyed orders.

The reunion was joyous. And I perceived a change in the fellowship. Just as the Rabbi had once predicted, they were now more cohesive, less suspicious, and happier.

But I still feared Simeon-of-the-knife.

Soon we were on the road again. The crowds that came to hear the Rabbi speak continued to grow in size. And throughout our journeys, I continued my writings.

I noticed a specific group appearing in our midst more often. Their clothing and mannerisms distinguished them from our usual followers. Little Simon explained that these were important people from the synagogue in Jerusalem.

I had often had reason to walk past that grand structure. It was an architectural wonder. A marketplace stood at the entrance where moneychangers accepted Roman coinage in exchange for the temple's. Animals could be purchased for the sacrifices—from sparrows to oxen—to either be slaughtered and burned in appeasement or to solicit a favour from Yahweh. The great I Am was said to live in the temple—specifically, in a room called the Holy of Holies. But only Jews were allowed into the temple. Gentiles enjoyed only limited access.

A multitude of pilgrims, Jews from other parts of Israel, and those living abroad came daily to this most sacred place. It was, I assumed, always crowded.

I also knew that the Romans suspected it to be more than a place for the people to meet with Yahweh. It was also a hotbed of turmoil, spawning seeds of rebellion. Within these walls, one could openly plot against the Roman Eagle.

Talk of rebelling against Rome and its taxes always troubled me. Rebellion was illogical. Did these Jews not realize how much it cost Rome to build, maintain, and patrol the roads, thus making them safe for pilgrims, traders, and other travellers? Pax Romana—a costly enterprise.

The Rabbi often sparred with the leaders who came from the synagogue. One day they challenged him over taxation—a loaded trick question. I was curious as to how the Rabbi would handle this. Would he be bested? I would have to report his answer verbatim, for I had been ordered to do so. I always obeyed orders.

In a brilliant manoeuvre, the Rabbi turned their trick question upside-down. He simply asked one of these men for a coin.

"Whose face is on the coin?" His voice was calm, nonchalant.

"Why, the emperor's of course," replied one of these elite men. I saw the disdain in his eyes.

The Rabbi returned the coin. "Then give to Caesar that which is due him. Give to God that which is due to God."

When he turned away, I wanted to congratulate him. None of my tutors in Alexandria would have been able to respond better. But it was not my place. I kept silent, although I did smile.

The growing rift between the Jewish leaders and the Rabbi caused me concern. I once heard him refer to these men as white-washed sepulchres: pretty on the outside, full of carrion on the inside. With words such as these, I feared the Rabbi was poking the wasp nest with a stick.

Those who followed the Rabbi were actually two distinct groups. Those who followed intermittently were known as disciples, whereas those who followed constantly were called apostles.

Simeon-of-the-knife was an apostle. Little Simon explained to me that Simeon was a zealot, a group that was very much anti-Rome. That's why he carried a knife. I wondered how many Roman throats he had slit. I still feared him.

I wondered why the Rabbi had singled out his apostles. Matthew, I learned, had been a hated tax collector. Little Simon said that the man had cheated his own people. Others were farmers. Judas came from a wealthy family. Then there was Big Simon and his brother Andrew, who were fishermen. I couldn't figure out why they had been chosen; there were no logical connections.

"My dad had been out on the boat with his brother all night," Little Simon told me one day. "You fish at night, because fish sleep deep in the sea during the day. Their nets all came up empty, meaning they earned no income after a night's work. While they were drying their nets—you have to do that, dry the nets—Jesus asked them why they weren't fishing. He was a carpenter visiting Capernaum and knew nothing about fish and their sleeping habits. My dad wanted to humour this stranger, so he took his boat out a bit and threw a net over. He shrugged to indicate what a waste of time and energy it was. But then, as he began to haul the net in, something weird happened. There were so many fish! My uncles had to bring their boats and nets. We'd be rich! So many fish! The carpenter then asked my dad, his brother, and their cousins to join him in catching people for Yahweh." The boy laughed. "Can you imagine Simeon caught in a net?"

"Without his knife?" I asked with a smirk.

Little Simon laughed all the harder.

Another day, the Rabbi asked whether I would be willing to tutor the children when they were in camp, but only in the evenings after I'd completed my work. Most came from a rural background and had few opportunities beyond their station.

I no longer found these children, who had once been so alien to me, so unpleasant. However, I only had a rudimentary knowledge of Jewish mores. There were so many, and they were so very complicated. I feared crossing boundaries since I was the stranger in their midst.

"Simeon can help." The Rabbi smiled brightly. "He knows *all* the taboos. Go ask him. Together you'll come up with a curriculum."

I was sure he must have seen me wince at the mention of my antagonist's name! I was not brave.

Smiling even more broadly, he added, "That's an order… you always obey orders."

Breathe, calm, focus. How many times did I do thus?

But I did approach Simeon-of-the-knife. We would never be friends, and he truly believed I was a Gentile spy, a wolf among the sheep. We did, however, compile a list of topics to cover, albeit a rather short one. Nothing on this list would offend the Torah or any religious conventions.

The Rabbi had taught me a lesson: you may not love your enemy, but you can peaceably co-exist.

I enjoyed instructing the children. I had never envisioned entering the role of a tutor. I also learned a second lesson from the Rabbi: teaching is difficult.

There was another incident regarding a dead person, and this time I was able to use my training to confirm that a death had indeed occurred.

While approaching a small village, we encountered a funeral procession. The burial rites of the culture made this obvious; there were paid professional mourners, a body wrapped according to prescribed standards, and a grief-stricken mother.

We halted. It was the respectful thing to do.

The Rabbi approached the grieving woman while I distanced myself from the others, since I was slaveborn and Gentile. I didn't wish to sully the funeral by my presence.

I was able to hear that the death was indeed very sad. The woman was recently widowed and now her only child, a teenaged boy, had died.

She had no other children and no one to support her. She would become a beggar on the streets.

"Darius, please come," the Rabbi called, apparently not worrying my presence might cause a disturbance. "Unbind the boy."

I had been given an order and I always obeyed orders. It wasn't for me to question an order! I assumed he asked me because of my medical background. He must think I was familiar with the sight, feel, and smell of a corpse.

I began the unbandaging. As I did so, I reflected on the fact that Jewish law even mandated how a body should be wrapped. I uncovered the face linen first and proceeded on. Lucien had taught me the tests used to determine whether death had occurred. These checks were instilled in my brain. Temperature to touch? Cold. Breath signs? Absent, undetectable. Chest movement? Absent. Pulse points? Absent. The lips? Blue. Eyes? Fixed and unresponsive to my finger's movement. The extremities? Signs of pooling. Reflexes? Absent. Rigor? Yes.

I ran through the gamut of tests. This lad? He was indeed dead.

The Rabbi disagreed.

Had I missed something? Sometimes it can be very difficult to distinguish death from a very deep sleep, so I reran the checklist. I was confident, absolutely confident, that this was a corpse. The boy was dead. Long dead. I had the training to prove it.

Nonetheless, the Rabbi spoke: "Wake up, son."

And it was so! The lad sat up… and he was very confused!

As for myself? I was more so! But as I watched, the boy's colour was returning. His eyes were no longer fixed. His mobility had been restored. He was alive!

"He was only asleep. Physicians, what do they know?" The Rabbi smiled and looked at me directly. Was this a moment of levity?

My head was unhinged. He *had been* dead! This was illogical. How would I report it?

But I had to. I always obeyed orders.

The crowds following the Rabbi grew larger. On one occasion, there were thousands, requiring a very large space far from the nearest town. But the Rabbi's message remained the same whether the crowd was large or small: peace, to be obtained through kindness toward all, with no expectation of reciprocity, forgiving those who trespassed against you; and since actions have consequences, Yahweh would forgive those who forgave others.

We were far from a market one day when the Rabbi advised everyone to eat. Judas, who carried the purse, pointed out the size of the gathered crowd. Could we afford food for such a multitude? What merchant would be able to supply an order this large?

He did have a valid point.

"We'll share," the Rabbi responded.

But there were only a few buns and pieces of fish. The one named Andrew had found a boy whose mother had demonstrated the foresight to pack her son a lunch. Apparently the crowd had not.

What the Rabbi did next defied not only logic but the rules of science and order. He raised his eyes in prayer to the great I Am, as he always did, and said, "Now let's eat. Distribute the food."

I know that two minus one is one. I know it. It's easily proven, a baby math operation.

But not in this case. After everyone was sated, there were leftovers! Illogical. What kind of person had this level of power over the fundamental laws of science? Who *was* this man? My brain ached.

I began to worry about the Rabbi's safety. I had to follow orders and report on the crowd's size. But nothing in the Rabbi's talks even hinted at insurrection. Even so, Rome was leery of such large gatherings. The people of this country had staged many uprisings in the past.

I worried over the rift between the Rabbi and these Jewish leaders, as they were a powerful lot. The Rabbi defied their strict food laws and challenged the logic of the Sabbath by healing on that day.

Actions do have consequences, I thought.

But I said nothing. It was not my place.

On another occasion, I was present when the Rabbi drew a literal line in the sand. The temple priests had condemned a young woman accused of adultery to death by stoning. The Rabbi stood by this line and proclaimed that only the person who had never sinned should pick up and toss the stones.

The accusers walked away.

I feared the Rabbi was on a collision course with the Jewish hierarchy. And once again I said nothing. It was not my place.

The physician in me saw that something was troubling the Master, for the eyes never lied. Was he... sad? Worried? Scared? Depressed? All of the above? He laughed, he prayed, he taught, he healed, and he ate... but I knew something was causing him great distress.

Lucien had taught me well. I recognized the signs.

The apostles and disciples didn't see what I saw. They weren't trained. Instead they were elated. Jubilant! Their spirits soared. Nothing could stop their Rabbi. He was famous!

We were due to make a trip down to a town called Bethany where three close friends of the Rabbi lived. It was among his favourite rest stops.

Lazarus, as yet unmarried, was successful in business and had two sisters living with him. Martha was an excellent cook; the other, Mary, was bright and charming. The Rabbi enjoyed the family's hospitality in his downtime.

While on the way, a messenger arrived and urged the Rabbi to come quickly. It turned out that Lazarus was ill... seriously ill. Martha and Mary were asking him to hurry, before it was too late.

But he didn't hurry. Instead what should have been a short trip dragged into a long one, even while the apostles reminded him of the need to speed up. The Rabbi dallied and took his time.

This delay troubled me. It was so unlike the Rabbi to casually ignore such an urgent request—and Lazarus was his friend!

Finally we approached Bethany, but it was too late. Lazarus had died and was buried according to Jewish burial laws within the required timespan.

Martha was angry and couldn't understand. The usually cheerful Mary was distraught and in deep grief.

Martha voiced what everyone was thinking.

"Now you show up?" she demanded.

The Rabbi asked to be shown where Lazarus had been interred. It was customary, I assumed, for him to show his respects to the deceased.

Everyone followed the sisters to the site. Others from the town followed along, and the size of the procession increased as they got closer.

I had learned much of the Jewish people's ways from Simeon, particularly the protocols regarding death and burial. Wealthy people purchased tombs cut into hillsides; the body would be wrapped and placed on a stone slab. After the prescribed waiting period, once the corpse had decomposed, the bones would be gathered and placed in a stone jar called an ossuary, to await the final judgment when body and spirit were to be reunited.

A rock had been rolled over the cut to Lazarus's tomb, but it was moveable. After all, someone did need to go back in and retrieve the bones at some point.

Was the Rabbi, in his guilt and grief, lost in a state of hysteria? As I watched, he shocked the bystanders by asking them to open the tomb—to move the massive stone. By now, I knew this would be considered an act of defilement. A Jewish person could not touch a corpse.

Was the Rabbi going to enter this tomb? That would be totally taboo!

Martha reminded the Rabbi that he had lost the opportunity to help Lazarus, who had now been entombed for four days.

But the Rabbi was adamant and ordered the two most able-bodied of his apostles, Simon and Simeon, to move the rock.

The Rabbi called out his friend's name: "Lazarus, wake up!"

There was a collective holding of breath. The gathering of people didn't make a sound.

And yet there *was* a sound—a stirring, a shuffling, a muddled voice…

"Jesus?"

"Darius, please," the Rabbi suddenly called. "The unwrapping… and carry out the checks. You have been trained. Now, please."

He was ordering me to enter the tomb! He wanted *me* to enter…? But I was not brave. I couldn't move. I was unable to move.

"Darius!" The Rabbi's voice was not angry, but it was more demanding this time. "I have given you an order."

I had to obey. I always obeyed.

The space did not smell of death, only of the myrrh, aloes, and spices used to prepare the corpse. And to my great shock, a figure stood before me like a spectre—Lazarus!

I had to be brave.

Breathe, calm, focus.

"Sir, it is I, Darius. The Rabbi has instructed me to unbind you. I mean you no harm."

As I began the unwrapping, my trained eye scanned the facial linen first. I performed all the checks. This man who had been four days dead—even if only in a deep sleep, he would have been deprived of food, water, and most certainly would have succumbed—was alive! Whoever read what I was about to scribe would surely doubt my sanity. At that moment, even I doubted my sanity!

Breathe, calm, focus.

The jubilant crowd moved on back to Bethany while I stood with the burial wraps in hand. My head ached! But I had to move, for I had orders to follow and a report to write. Even in this confused state, I always obeyed orders.

News of such an event could not be contained. Lazarus was a well-respected, well-known figure. No trickery was afoot. Lazarus had no guile in him, and neither did his sisters.

The Rabbi too was famous! Some were calling him a king, which greatly disturbed me. Rome had only one emperor and would not tolerate talk of another within her territories.

As the disciples' and apostles' elation grew, I couldn't help diagnosing that the Rabbi did not share their enthusiasm. His eyes revealed the truth; they were deeply troubled.

I was too.

It was nearing the time of the Passover, a great Jewish religious holiday. Little Simon had explained it to me. The occasion marked the night when the long-enslaved Jewish people had been set free to return to their long-forgotten homeland of Israel.

They had been enslaved in Egypt for a very long time, the young master taught me. There was to have been one last sign before their release. During the night, the Angel of Death took the lives of the first-born, human and animal—and in the morning, with so many young dead, the Pharaoh finally let the Jewish slaves leave.

But the Angel had needed to know in which homes the Jewish children, and dogs too, lived. So that none of the Jews would die, their leader Moses told them to kill a sheep and smear blood on the door. The sheep meat was then to be cooked and eaten as everyone readied themselves for travel. They had to leave fast!

Once Pharaoh realized that he'd let all the workers go, he sent soldiers out to bring the slaves back. But his soldiers drowned in the Red Sea, for Moses had parted the water only for the Jewish people.

Little Simon was proud to tell me his people's history and the importance of the holiday. Passover was fast approaching.

The group too was fast approaching. They were, by now, ready to enter Jerusalem.

As the Rabbi sat upon a donkey, the crowds inside the city were so excited that they laid palms to form a green carpet for the humble animal to walk. All the while, they chanted, "The king of the Jews! Hosanna in the highest!"

I was well-distanced. I was a Gentile. However, I prayed to whatever god of slaveborns might be listening.

Please, please silence these people…

But that god ignored my pleas.

The city was crammed with Jews both from across Israel and abroad. The coming Passover was to be a most special feast; the high priest would be in contact with the great I Am in a room called the Holy of Holies, according to Little Simon, and at the appointed hour the lambs and oxen would be slaughtered, their bodies burning on altars in honour of Yahweh.

In order for Jews to partake in the rituals and festivities, they must also strictly avoid contact with Gentiles… something to do with defilement. Therefore, I wouldn't see him or Simi for a few days. These people had many social and religious mores to observe.

I returned to Antonia Fortress, to the small cell located off the centurion's office. Upon the desk were many forms, requisitions, and letters to be translated and sent on to Rome. This work calmed me and kept me focused. I couldn't afford to be "away." I needed the structure.

I was barely settled when two guards from the governor's palace came for me. They roughly escorted me out onto the street and took me to the governor's private residence. Up until now, I hadn't been too worried. But what was this about? Did it have to do with some translation business?

I looked around the private residence, wondering whether the guards had made some mistake in bringing me here.

They hadn't. I was forced toward a door and pushed into a very sumptuous chamber. I was more than unsettled.

Breathe, calm, focus.

A grand-looking woman sat on a typical but very plush Roman-style lounge—and when she spoke to the guards, her voice was imperious.

"You may leave."

The lead guard seemed surprised. "My lady?"

"Leave! And when I require your assistance, I will call."

Both guards glared at me, but they obeyed.

The door closed.

"You are the scribe, Darius?" Her voice was much softer, less haughty than before.

With my eyes and head in the proper position, I replied in my best slave-speak: "Yes, my lady."

"Approach," she said almost in a whisper. "Come closer."

She patted the lounge and motioned for me to approach.

Now I was indeed very, very unsettled. At first I didn't move.

"I said, come here!" she repeated herself, sounding more threatening.

I gulped. *Breathe, calm, focus…*

That was an order. I always obeyed orders.

I moved closer.

She patted the lounge. "Sit!"

My head was thumping… or was it my heart? Perhaps both.

"My la—"

"Sit! I don't bite. I am Claudia, the governor's wife. We must be discreet. There are spies everywhere, fools who can be bought off for a jug of wine. Sit."

Breathe, calm, focus. I sat.

Claudia lifted my chin. I winced, feeling startled.

She stifled a laugh. "I like to look people in the eyes. Eyes never lie."

My eyes opened wide!

"You have the ear of the one called the Rabbi?" she demanded.

I let my mouth run away from my brain. "Only in the capacity of a physician, my lady."

Claudia had to stifle a laugh. "You must get word to him. His life is in great danger—not from Rome, but from his own people, the leaders of his own nation. They want him silenced. As I said, spies are everywhere. Even one of his closest followers is involved. There is a credible plot. My husband Pontius tells me everything. He… he is a good man and has resisted action so far. But my husband is weak, and there is talk, *threats*, that this matter will reach Augustus. Pontius will capitulate to the emperor and choose to secure his own job over saving the Rabbi's life. You must tell him to leave the city immediately." She took a deep breath. "Darius, did he—the Rabbi, I mean—restore life to the dead? Is he the one whom the Jews call the Messiah? I have read your reports."

I gulped. "I have little knowledge of the term *Messiah*. I am a proficient physician." I gulped again. "I performed the death checks on two people." Another gulp. "It's illogical, so very illogical… they were indeed well dead. Yet now they live."

"You must warn him!"

Suddenly, the woman's head moved, as though sensing something unseen. With a finger, she gestured for me to return to my original spot in the middle of the room. I stood there, eyes lowered, and bowed in submission.

"Guards!" Claudia called in her imperial voice.

As the guards entered, she began to berate me, not loudly but most emphatically. "If I ever hear of you harassing one of my staff again, it'll be more than a tongue-lashing you'll receive! Now out, all of you!"

The guards escorted me out of the room and then hauled me outside to the palace gate. I wasn't prepared for their intensity. One held my shoulders tightly while the other punched his fist into my stomach. I sprawled to the ground as one of them delivered an emphatic kick of his boot to drive home his message.

"Lady Pilate let you off easy," he growled. "This you will remember." Another blow.

Moments later, they were gone.

It was difficult to breathe, and instinctively I began a self-examination. Tender area? No broken ribs. Pulse point? Racy, but present. Diagnoses? No major damage. I was winded and there would be bruising. The patient would survive.

I hoped that the guard's fist would hurt as much as my abdomen, that both of us would be in pain. The whole incident was for naught, for I had never "harassed" anyone.

I needed to sit, to let my pulse steady and allow the air to return. The immediate blow would soften given time.

My mind went deep into memory and recalled a conversation I'd had with Lucien, perhaps as a teenager.

"Darius, what are the two most important organs in any body?"

A baby question. "The heart and brain, sir."

"And which of these two is the prime force?"

Lucien was asking the impossible. Both were prime: if either one stopped, the entire system shut down. In what direction was this lesson headed?

"Sir?"

"Darius, you are what some, both male and female, may consider attractive."

My face reddened. I had never considered my appearance as anything more than an outward shape.

"Sir?"

I still didn't understand. I could deduce no connection between these subjects—the heart, the brain, and my outward appearance.

Lucien could see my confusion, for he accurately read my eyes. "For most people, the heart is the prime controller. Often outward attraction is the first to set the controller into action, like the starting of a machine. Most people will form bonds, affections, friendships, and companionships which will be pleasant and long-lasting. Most will find contentment that way, even dying surrounded by their grandchildren.

"Yes, you have a heart. You must never—let me stress, *never*—let your heart rule your brain. That's for others to do, but not for you. Should you forget or ignore this lesson and allow your heart to rule, you will surely fall into despair, grief… madness. It will lead to your ruination. I saw you early on. Despite your low birth, you possess one of those rare brains. Remember how I called you a sponge when you were a child?"

"I do, sir."

I also remembered the teasing I had received when my cohorts had dunked me into puddles.

"Some sponges are small," said Lucien. "They are somewhat useful. They're capable of minimal absorption. Most are average-sized, capable of more. Your brain is capable of ever so much. How much remains to be seen. Yours is a rare brain. So you must always, *always*, allow your brain to control your heart. You must absorb, hypothesize, analyze, deduce, infer, speculate, and reach a logical conclusion. Only in this way will you ever survive in sanity. Eros, philia, storge, and agape… these are for others, not for you. It may sound hard. It is. But that's the reality of it—you are slaveborn. Head, not heart. I hope I've made my point."

"You have, sir."

Lucien had given me advice I never forgot later in life.

As I lay sprawled on the ground outside the palace gates, I renewed my hope that the guard who'd hit me had broken a knuckle or two.

I managed to rise and began taking the first painful steps away from the palace.

I slept poorly that night. With the bruising, I couldn't get physically comfortable. My brain would not settle. A heavy burden had been placed on my shoulders. I had to find a way to warn the Rabbi of the plot... that one of his own was part of it. But how? It was Passover, and I was a Gentile.

I heard talk that the Rabbi was to speak within the temple walls. Meanwhile, my desk was clear. Indeed, the entire military had been placed on high alert, leaving me with little to do.

Perhaps I could contact him before he entered the synagogue? The weight of Pilate's wife's words felt heavy.

I had to find the Rabbi.

Too late, I learned that there had been an altercation at the marketplace. The Rabbi had upended the tables of the moneychangers. Roman coins and Jewish shekels scattered everywhere as the Rabbi called them cheats. He had opened pens to free sheep and oxen, even freeing sparrows from their cages. The sacrificial animals were loose. The Rabbi had berated the vendors for turning his Father's house into a public concourse.

Apparently the Rabbi was very angry.

I searched the crowds outside the temple, searching for a familiar face. Where were the disciples? The apostles? The Marys? Salome?

The kitchen, of course! Salome was a Jewess. That was the most likely place to find her.

I went to the governor's kitchen and no one stopped me, for I had been seen around the palace. The kitchen girls even seemed pleased to see me.

"Look who's here," one of them remarked playfully as she approached; I realized that this was an example of *levity*. "We've missed you."

My face reddened and I forced myself to sound calm. "Is Salome present, mistresses?"

"She's got Passover off." This girl smiled. "Maybe I can help?" she sidled up.

Was this too levity?

"No," I said, stopping her. "Thank you for your time, mistresses."

Where to now? I had an order, and I always obeyed orders. I certainly needed to obey this order. A life depended on it! My failures had already caused so many deaths.

The Roman troops around the city were on high alert. I continued my search, listening for any information I could glean. It seemed that the Rabbi was still safe but was continuing to face off against his nation's highest leaders. I even heard something about him seeking to destroy the temple and rebuild it in three days?

I feared the Rabbi was in ever greater danger.

On late Thursday afternoon, the crowds on the streets were thinning. The people were returning to their homes to prepare the ritualistic meal.

Just as I was beginning to despair, I saw two familiar faces! Two of the Rabbi's disciples.

But they weren't too pleased to see me. After all, I was a Gentile and Passover was fast approaching. They feared defilement.

I told them what Pilate's wife had discovered: a plot devised by the Pharisees, high priests, and elders to silence the Rabbi. I also warned that one of the apostles was a traitor, and that Pilate would capitulate. The Rabbi, for his safety, should leave the city immediately.

They had to believe this was not a rumour, that the governor's wife was a friend. But I had obeyed an order, delivered the warning, and satisfied the burden; I no longer felt it weighing down my shoulders.

As I watched, the two disciples entered a building and climbed to the upper room that the group had been using for preparations while in Jerusalem. I didn't know whether they would share my words or not, but I prayed to the Rabbi's God that they would. I prayed that he would be safe.

I returned to the fortress, where I was confined to my cell unless my presence was requested during the evening hours. I had no knowledge of the events that were transpiring, including the Rabbi's arrest by the temple guard.

At least I had obeyed an order.

On Friday morning, I awoke early and completed my ablutions. I was not yet at my desk, and already I felt unnerved.

Hearing a knock on my cell's door, I turned and immediately encountered centurion Marcus Longinus. He had never before entered my personal space and I felt terrified. I was not brave. Something was so very wrong.

I stood and repeated my mantra to myself: *Breathe, calm, focus.* My eyes lowered and my head bowed. I was more than unsettled.

"Darius, today will be a difficult day…" He hesitated. "For both of us. There will be three executions. I must attend, and so must you—in two capacities, scribe and physician."

The centurion placed a small flask upon my desk.

"Drink this," he instructed. "It will help calm the nerves. Make yourself ready, for we'll depart soon. The carpenters are already preparing the site."

Next he handed me instructions for three signs. I was also to prepare some drugged wine.

Once he'd left, I looked at the flask and decided that was one order I would disregard. Lucien had instilled in me the importance of remaining clear-ended at the most stressful of times: no alcohol, no drugs, and no sedatives.

Today I was confused, frightened, unhinged, and in turmoil, but I would forever remain clear-headed.

I rose. I had an order. And I almost always obeyed orders. I was clear-headed but smouldering inside as I glanced at the flask, resting unopened on the desk.

I prepared the signs which my master had asked of me, although one was slightly altered. I also prepared the drugged wine, using more than the allotted amount of the costly sedative. I knew what I was doing. I was stealing.

PART TWO

The End

I had obeyed my orders and drugged the wine which would be served.
I always obeyed orders. Well, almost always.

There would be consequences, for the words omitted from the
sign and for my "mismeasurements" in preparing the drugged wine. But
my fear of punishment in this moment paled in the face of this opportunity to help my friend.

"Darius!"

I looked toward the centurion, who sounded angry with my tardiness. He was waiting for me to bring the wine.

I had to be brave, not a strong trait in my character, as I approached
the cross. The wooden beam still lay on the ground and the Rabbi rested
upon it. The crucifixion was only just the beginning.

The Rabbi was quiet and almost accepting of his fate. I remembered
his words. He had called himself like a lamb brought to the slaughter.
He was bruised and bloodied. He had been whipped—from my training, I recognized the marks—and a hideous twine of brambles had been
stuffed onto his head.

"Darius! Get on with it or you'll be the next one to go…"

My master's voice trailed off and I had to wonder whether he was
upset with me. Or perhaps he was upset at himself. He was hard to read.

I knelt beside the Rabbi.

"It's me, Darius, sir." I took the sleeve of my tunic, wiped away some
of the dirt and blood from his face and held the wine to his lips. "Please,
Rabbi, drink this. It will help."

Calm, stay calm, I ordered myself. I always obeyed orders.

"It will help with the pain," I said. "I made it extra strong, to ease…"

His head turned away.

"Rabbi?" I prompted.

"Give it to the others, my friend."

My friend? My head spun at his words. *How can he call me his friend? I'm helping his executioners!*

He turned toward me. "Go to the others. Help them."

I had been given an order and I always obeyed orders. I stood up and walked to the other two men nailed to their crosses.

"Darius!" My master was calling again. "The signs."

I had been given the names of these convicted men and the crimes for which they were to be executed. I had prepared the signs on which words were written in three languages; they would be nailed above each man's head prior to the lifting of the crosses. The scaffolding had already been erected.

I was a good scribe, proficient in many languages, so this was an easy task for me. Nonetheless, I had altered the words that would appear above the Rabbi's head:

Jesus the Nazarene: King of the Jews

There would be repercussions for this. Actions always had consequences. But at this moment, I didn't really care.

I handed the signs, neatly written, to my master. He read the first two, then paused at the third. He knew what I had done.

I couldn't read his face—again, he was a hard one to read—but I thought I may have seen a hint of a smile.

One of the soldiers lifted his boot and struck Simi, who had ventured too close. I quickly intervened.

"Pardon, sir, allow me to remove the beast," I said to the soldier using my very best slave-speak. "You have more pressing matters. Allow me."

He backed away while the dog crept forward and licked the Rabbi's face. I then leaned down and picked Simi up.

"It's okay," I whispered.

I knew it wasn't, but I had to say something; the dog was shaking. I held him close, for comfort, but was it for the dog's or mine? I wasn't sure.

Simi just whimpered.

That's when I made a realization. Where was Big Simon? What about Simeon-of-the-knife? And the others, the Rabbi's many followers? Where were they?

I looked toward the crowd and spotted the two Marys. Then I spotted another woman, his mother's sister, and young John. John was standing as close to the hill as the guards would allow.

Turning my attention back to the scene, I realized that I would have to remain there until the end, which could take many hours. I was required to declare all three men dead.

I needed to focus. Thinking helped. It muffled the sound of hammering, the screams...

I needed to go "away," to keep myself sane. So I went, digging deep in my memory, determined to go to the beginning, to edit and analyze my responsibility for the events that had resulted in the Rabbi's execution...

Suddenly my mind was shocked back to reality—and found myself looking up at the hill, where the crosses had been erected. How long had I been "away"?

A dark cloud covered the sun and the air grew cold. A stiff wind was picking up.

Simi was still in my arms, still shaking, but this time from the cold.

And then I heard a voice. The Rabbi was speaking. Even now, under these circumstances, his voice was perfectly audible. He was speaking to his mother and John.

I swallowed hard, knowing the drill.

Breathe, calm, focus.

Even in such agony, so close to the end, the Rabbi was worried about his mother.

A few minutes later, there came another utterance. The Rabbi was speaking to his Father, Yahweh.

"Why have you forsaken me?" the man called to the heavens.

I thought the same. Why was this happening? Where was this Yahweh Father?

Another utterance; the Rabbi was thirsty, meaning it was my time to act. I placed Simi on the ground and soaked a sponge—how ironic, a sponge in the hands of one once called Sponge—until it was well wetted with the myrrh-hyssop mix.

An ever-efficient soldier approached and stood at my side. He tied the drugged sponge to a long pole and raised it to the Rabbi's lips.

It was over.

I was trained. I knew the signs.

It was now midafternoon and the earth trembled. I returned the dog to my arms. Was this it, the final judgment that the Rabbi had spoken of? Actions had consequences.

The shuddering ceased.

The Romans weren't totally cruel—ever efficient, definitely; cruel, not entirely—and the soldiers decided that it was time for this to end.

I had never witnessed a crucifixion. I had, however, heard of the procedure. To end the life of a criminal strung to the cross, the legs were to be broken. I understood the logistics. No longer able to support the body's weight on the foot peg, the body would hang, quickly causing the lungs to empty and the heart to stop.

Death.

And that was my last duty—to confirm that the Rabbi and the other two had passed. I wasn't the base physician. I was a scribe. Why me? There was another physician in the barracks. There was much paperwork, many forms to fill, but first a physician had to verify that death had indeed occurred. It fell on me to declare all three dead.

"Darius!" It was the centurion.

I placed Simi down. "Please don't run off," I said, hoping the dog understood.

I approached the first body. I was always amazed at how quickly a body alters after death.

I shall certainly require several washings after this, I thought to myself as I raised my arm. *Breathe, calm, focus.*

I began the death checks. This one—dead.

Breathe, calm, focus.

The second one—dead.

I struggled to maintain my composure. Lucien's voice was in my head: "You now have two patients. His mother is present."

I had to be professional as I approached the Rabbi's body.

He was dead, passed.

I didn't order what came next, for he was already dead. I don't know why, but the efficient soldier by my side raised his lance upward and pierced the Rabbi's side. He didn't need to. The Rabbi was dead. I was trained to recognize the signs.

"Darius, come," my master ordered.

I approached him in the proper position, with my eyes and head lowered.

"The paperwork can wait," he said. His voice was not unkind. "No rush. This has been difficult for both of us. Take as much time as you need. Leave."

Leave! Where?

"Yes, sir," I replied in the best slave-speak I could muster.

I felt shaken to the core. Where would I go?

Once again I heard Lucien in my head, and he was yelling: *"Head, never heart!"*

I approached the Rabbi's mother and offered the only word I could manage. "Sorry." I couldn't even string a sentence together. In my head, I feebly added, *I was just following orders.*

"Thank you, Darius," she said.

In all Mary had witnessed, in her profound grief, she was thanking me? I simply nodded, my eyes and head properly lowered.

"Perhaps you would be so kind as to return Simi," John said.

I looked down, remembering that I still held the dog in my arms.

I gulped. It had been many hours now and Little Simon would be worried.

"Of course, sir, right away."

Breathe, calm, focus.

"You know where to find the boy?" John asked.

"In the upper room, sir?" I was finding it hard to speak. Why are these people being so nice to me?

"Yes," John replied. "But they are terrified, all of them. There's a code. Knock once, then wait, knock three more times, then knock once more. Someone will unbolt the door."

"I understand, sir."

I left the hill known as Calvary, Golgotha, a.k.a. the place of the skull. I hoped I would never see this place again.

I did as instructed and proceeded with Simi to the upper room. Following an order made sense and helped me restore balance to my world.

Returning to the barracks, I fell into a daily routine of work, sitting at my desk and shuffling between parchments, forms, and requisitions. I had my ducks all in a row. Work kept me sane. I needed the structure. There was no chance to get "away"; there was only work.

There would be retribution, though. My actions would have consequences. A myrrh shortage would be discovered. It was too valuable an item to go unnoticed. Then there were the words I'd omitted on the Rabbi's sign…

Yes, actions had consequences.

But no one questioned either the herb shortage or the carelessly scribed board. There was no retribution. Curious! Romans were usually so very efficient.

A week passed, perhaps, and the routine of work quieted my mind. Everything made sense. It was logical. Two minus one equalled one. As I sat at my desk, I controlled the stylus, the flow of the ink. Work kept me sane.

If the multitudinous forms and translations which comprised my duties were completed before the end of each workday, I would move my desk outside the cell and make my scribe service available to the soldiers. Most, though fine in their line of work, were illiterate. Often they would request that I write letters home for them, a service I was pleased to offer. It must have been comforting to know that someone was awaiting their return. Some said "Thank you," which from a freeborn was payment in itself. Others offered a few coins to show appreciation. I had free access to supplies, so I had no need of money. I'd politely lower my head and say, "No need, sir."

The door to the cell where I worked and slept was always open during working hours. The centurion might call me to come at any time. As such, I couldn't help but hear the soldiers' conversation.

One day I heard my master's optio—his second-in-command—laughing. A boy about so high had presented himself at the gate "requesting entrance" for an "urgent audience" with centurion Marcus Longinus on "a matter of great importance." Those were all his words, followed by bursts of fresh laughter in turn.

The optio composed himself. It seemed that the sentries gathered around him were quite amused.

"This lad at the gate is quite determined," the optio to the centurion. "One of the sentries came to get me. He thought I'd get a chuckle. The boy stresses that he needs to see you on a matter of utmost importance. A life seems to be at stake. And the boy is so sincere, so brave and determined… well, he'd make a fine soldier if he weren't a Jew. What do you want me to do?"

"Send the boy in," the centurion announced. "A life is at stake and I have time. I need a diversion."

I knew it had to be Little Simon.

"Darius, come!" My master's voice was hard to read. "This young lad needs medical assistance."

Immediately I left my desk and entered the office. As expected, there was Little Simon, looking up at the soldiers expectantly.

"It's my dog, sir," said Little Simon. "He's poorly."

We didn't look at each other. Was Simi ill?

"You have any experience with dogs?" The optio asked, suppressing his laughter.

"Yes, sir, I have some experience."

"Take what you need and go tend to this… emergency." The centurion's tone was unusually flat. "Finish your duties when you return."

I lowered my eyes. "Yes, sir."

"Pups over paper… isn't that the great Caesar's slogan?" The optio roared with laughter again. He found this very entertaining.

I gathered a few supplies, then left the barracks and fell into step next to Little Simon. We didn't speak until we were well beyond the gate.

"I think I lied," Little Simon said, sounding worried. "Simi's fine. But I needed a way to get you to come. It was the only excuse I could think of. Do you think Yahweh is mad?" He looked so contrite.

"Not at all, young master. You used logic to formulate a ruse and you executed it in fine style. You showed initiative."

How, I wondered, could any god not admire this?

We went to the very same upper room where I had deposited Simi; it seemed like a lifetime ago, but only ten days had actually passed since *that day*.

The signal was given and the door unbarred. After we entered, the door was securely fastened behind us.

Inside, I found that the shutters were closed. The dark room was lit only by candles and my eyes quickly adjusted. I glanced down and saw the wiggly Simi yipping at my feet.

"Shalom, Darius." It was a young girl's voice and I turned to see mistress Olivia, with whom I'd previously enjoyed many a debate. "Come, Mother Mary wishes to speak with you."

I felt Olivia's small hand take mine. She hadn't grown much. She would not be tall.

"I'm sorry I used to argue with you," she remarked.

We couldn't avoid eye contact; my gaze was lowered, as was proper, and hers was raised, as was needed.

I had to stop, though, for her words had disarmed me. I had to kneel to her level. Somehow we were equals, since she had frequently bested me.

"Mistress Olivia, we do not argue," I insisted. "We debate, and sometimes you outmanoeuvre me. There is no need for an apology. I sense that you have, as I was once told, a rather large sponge-brain."

That made her giggle.

"It's a wonderful gift," I added, and I meant it.

As she led me toward where the others were seated, I felt a pang of regret that it seemed her life would be difficult. This was a very patriarchal society.

I came up to Mary, the Rabbi's mother, who had a stool placed before her. She motioned for me to sit.

I hesitated. "My lady, it is not—"

"Sit!"

I glanced up at the speaker—none other than Simeon-of-the-knife. With an involuntary wince, I sat.

Mary took my hands into hers. I was uncomfortable with touch, for she still unnerved me.

"Remember when we talked in Capernaum, just the two of us?" Her voice was as soft and gentle as ever. "Please, look up, Darius. It's okay. It's an order. You always obey orders."

The physician in me noticed that her eyes looked somehow *different*. Were they radiant?

"Yes, my lady, I do." I tried to look down.

Suddenly, unexpectedly, she reached out and tousled my hair. I had no experience with such a gesture, for no one had ever done that to me. The sensation was new.

Then her fingers ran along my cheeks and I recoiled in total shock. Next, her fingers gently rubbed the notch in my ear. Was this what a mother's touch felt like?

She let out a soft laugh. "You are indeed a little sparrow. Remember when I told you I was normal and you said you thought neither me nor my son were normal, that we were otherborn? And remember Gabriel the angel? And remember the part of the story where Joseph married me knowing the child growing in me wasn't his? Well, have you heard the term man-god?"

As unsettled as I felt, she had asked a question. I was obliged to respond.

"Yes, my lady. Pharaohs, emperors, and kings often refer to themselves as such. In one culture, long ago, a human would be selected, gilded with real gold, placed on a throne, exalted, and honoured. Of course he didn't live long, this man-god. He couldn't eat or drink, and he had to inhale the toxic fumes from the melted gold. The man-god lived but a few days."

"This is a bit different," Mary continued. "Please, look up. It's okay. The Jews have an ages-long connection with the so-called "disembodied spirits" that come to variously help or cause chaos. They were the great I Am's first creation. Yahweh was content, as you would say, but can an architect hold back from designing? Can a musician stop himself from playing? I Am first caused these disembodied spirits to be. Then Yahweh gave these spirits, these angels, the gift of free choice. Unencumbered by physical limitations, they possessed great power. Some chose to live in harmony with I Am; others chose another path, to set themselves up as angel-gods. I Am then created the cosmos, the earth, all the creatures seen and unseen, and the plants and waters needed to sustain them. Yahweh breathed life into His newest angels, angels with bodies; he called them humans and also gave them the gift of free choice. But humans sinned, breaking the one simple rule given by I Am.

"The leader of those angel-gods who found themselves cast from I Am's sight goes by many names—Satan, Legion, Devil… whatever his name, he lays claim to humanity, calling them the spawn of sin. So Yahweh promised to send one who would make these wrongs right. Since a human first erred, a human must come as their redeemer—not a man-god, but God-in-man."

Everyone was silent. The room was dark, and I felt unsettled. I wanted to be back at my desk. But I remained seated. I had been ordered to sit.

"Darius, that's my son," Mary added. "That's why Jesus was born. That's why he did all the illogical things he did. But not before raising his eyes to Yahweh, his Father. That's why he died. It wasn't an order; it was his mission."

Mary once again stroked my cheeks. All the while I remained motionless. It was hard to breathe, let alone find calm. I tried to focus.

"Oh, Sparrow, if you only knew how loved you are, how special you are!" she murmured. "You're like the oyster. Your shell is hard and gnarled. Your life has been difficult. You've lived at the bottom of the sea with creatures nibbling at your shell. But inside the oyster? A beautiful, precious pearl.

"There is one more thing. For now, I'll remain here with the disciples, but later Mary Magdelene and I will go to Capernaum to stay with John's kin. While I'm in Jerusalem, I'll be available should you want to talk. But remember that centurions do get reassigned, and at some point you also will be sent away.

"Your brain must be in disorder right now, so this will be hard for you to grasp. You are so logical, Darius, but my son lives! Really lives. Like Lazarus, who was four days dead, he lives in body and spirit. He has been resurrected."

As several others in the room gathered around us, the physician in me diagnosed hysteria. What Mary said was illogical and incredulous.

"We've all seen him," Big Simon said.

"I touched his hands," the disciple named Thomas insisted. "I felt the place where the nails were driven through his wrists. I felt the opening where the lance pierced his side. I felt a real body!"

"He's eaten with us," Little Simon proclaimed with enthusiasm. "I watched him do it. If the Rabbi were a ghost, the food would've just dropped on the floor and Simi would've had a snack. The food stayed inside!"

I had to respond to the little master, for I had grown quite fond of him. "You were wise to watch. Very logical."

Breathe, I reminded myself. *You must breathe. You must calm. You must focus. They are all hysterical... this is mass hysteria...*

The beautiful Mary Magdelene sensed my discomfort and grazed my shoulder. "You have seen so many illogical things, Darius. The blind seeing, the deaf hearing, the lepers cleansed. You even pronounced two people dead only for them to rise. But they live. Illogical? But they live. Why is this so different, so hard for you to comprehend?"

"Darius will need time and space to process this," said the Rabbi's mother. "His brain requires time to understand."

At that moment, I certainly didn't understand these people, nor the words they spoke. I doubted I ever would understand.

Salome came to the rescue. "I know you must get back. The centurion will be sending out a search party." She gave me a big hug. "Shalom, Darius. I hope… I pray you will find peace."

I said nothing.

I was about to leave when I remembered why I had agreed to come in the first place—to examine Simi. True, Little Simon had admitted his excuse was a ruse, but I would not have the young master fretting about whether some angry god would seek to punish him for his lie. So I would give the dog an exam—ergo, no lie. I didn't want to feel any more guilt.

Salome placed a blanket on the table and I conducted a full physical exam of the puppy. I asked Little Simon about Simi's food, water, and elimination habits; he giggled at this. I then withdrew a vial containing honey and allowed the dog to lick my fingers.

There, the medicine was administered. There was no lie.

"Young master Simon, the examination is complete," I announced. "You may lift your dog down and resume your activities."

Just as I was about to leave, I felt a tug on my tunic. I looked down into the wide eyes of mistress Olivia.

"Darius?" she said. "Did you… did you ever get teased?"

I knelt to her level. She would never be tall. "Yes, young mistress, even to this day."

"How did you handle it? I get so angry! I want to hit them. That would be wrong, though." She sighed. "They call me a baby…"

"And how would you describe a baby?"

"Cute and cuddly."

"And?"

Olivia brightened. "And everyone loves them."

"My tutor long ago told me to consider the teasing as levity," I told her. "The ones who tease are perhaps dissatisfied with their lot in life. They are teasing you to brighten the drudgery of their own lives. It hurts, yes. Teasing hurts. But your tormentors are in need of levity. Perhaps it's all part of having a sponge-brain."

As she smiled at this, I knew her life would be difficult.

"I sense Mary Magdelene has some wisdom," I said in a soft voice." Perhaps you should seek her counsel."

The girl looped her arms around my neck. "I'm sorry you never knew your mother," she whispered.

"Me too, little mistress. Thank you. You have taught me much. Shalom."

My head was banging as I departed the upper room. If my brain were truly as large as Lucien had once claimed, then surely it was now trying to escape. I had absorbed too much. It was all just too much. Too much touch… too many words… I needed structure. I needed my desk. I needed order. I needed routine.

I suddenly realized I was in an unfamiliar neighbourhood of the city.

"Damn!" I said, realizing I must have taken a wrong turn.

"Now that's one expletive I never would have expected to come out of a sparrow's mouth."

I recognized that voice and knew I'd become totally unhinged. I must have fallen and hit my head. Was I concussed? Was I, in fact, dead?

I felt the sensation of touch, a hand on my shoulder. It had never been a comfortable feeling for me. Until recently, I'd had very little experience with touch or that kind of familiarity.

I winced. The hand was removed. I didn't move. I was frozen.

"Come, Darius. Like my mother said, we need to talk. Isn't she remarkable! And yes, that is what a mother's touch feels like… like the touch of Yahweh. A loving touch that seeks to wipe away every pain and disappointment, to protect from every danger and illness. But it's not the mother's journey."

Breathe, calm, focus.

Nothing.

"I know I once said that birds will rest in the mustard seed bush. But Darius, I'm not asking you to sit in a tree… it's only a bench. Come, sit."

His voice sounded normal. Perhaps even amused.

I still couldn't move.

"You realize I could physically cause you to move?" There was levity in his voice.

I felt no levity. I was frozen.

"I command you to sit."

Well, I had been issued an order, loud and clear. Instinctively I moved. I sat on the nearby bench. I always obeyed.

"Thanks for being there." He moved closer and playfully bumped my shoulder; I felt it. "I know how obsessive you are. I appreciated that gesture, wiping my face." He laughed. "Bet your tunic got a good scrubbing afterward!"

He took something out of the side pocket of his robe. A handful of figs.

"Want one?" he offered. "I do enjoy figs. I felt badly for cursing that tree. I was hungry, but it had no fruit. Such a human reaction. Want one?"

"No, sir, I am—"

"I know," he said, cutting me off. "You're content. But you're not, are you?"

He reached out and *pinched* me with his fingers.

"I'm not a hallucination. You are not in a dreamlike state. You're not concussed. You felt that. You reacted. It was a reflex. This is real. I'm a physician too. You *reacted*."

I did react! Turning to face him, I let my mouth run away with my brain and blurted out in an uncharacteristically loud voice, "You always spoke about a loving Father. Some Father. You even called out to him at the end. You called out to him and—"

"I was in pain! Lots of pain! Unbearable pain. Really, Darius, you of all people must have realized that. It was so much for the human side of me to endure. That utterance was a normal human reaction."

Had I crossed a line? He sounded angry. I couldn't look at him.

Suddenly, I realized that I had been looking directly at him, making eye contact. And it was truly him—the Rabbi. Instinctively I lowered my eyes and bowed my head, as was proper for one in my position.

"Darius, my Father did hear me. He did respond." The Rabbi no longer sounded angry. "There was a cloud, an earthquake, and a torn carpet-door in the temple…"

"You cured others," I mumbled. "You made enough food to feed thousands. You did the illogical! But you let them… no, it's all so illogical…"

"It was my mission! I accepted it… my human side, I accepted it. Actions have consequences. I knew the consequences." He sounded angry again. "You have no idea of the consequence of my choice. Legion lay claim to the embodied angels—humans, you would call them—arguing that since the disembodied angels had been cast from Yahweh's sight for their arrogance and desire for power, so should humanity now, in the name of justice. For humans also lust after power and are equally sinful. It was my choice to do this. I outplayed Satan. He knew of Yahweh and I Am. Legion never considered me, never considered the consequences of my choice to restore justice."

The Rabbi's tone softened and he playfully bumped my shoulder again.

"I freely accepted my mission. I am, you know, freeborn," he continued. "Lucien tells me that your work so far has been *adequate*. That's the word he used. And he has one lesson he wants you to remember, while your brain is processing all this. He wants you to remember the horse on backing day…"

I was still a new teen, still very angry and sullen—feelings that were unfamiliar to me. Lucien and I had gone to the stud farm. We went there frequently as both horse and rider often required the services of a physician. We had no patient this time; it was a backing day, when the young horses were to be introduced to a saddle and a rider's weight. The farm raised and sold horses for that purpose.

We stood outside a round pen. The posts were stout, the cross boards high. I watched a young horse be led in; it was accustomed to a halter and lead. A long tether was attached to a pole in the middle of the ring, and the other end connected to the young animal.

"Watch the body language," said Lucien. "Animals do communicate. Watch the eyes, ears, tail, body language… horse-speak."

The animal tried to escape, but it was tethered. It was prancing and pawing. Suddenly, a burst of energy! It ran in circles and the rope wrapped itself around the pole tighter and tighter until it was trapped.

"Watch the eyes. So wide. The whites are showing. The ears are flat back."

A groom approached and the horse tried to move away, but there was no escape. The saddle was placed on its back, then a strap tightened. With another burst, the horse started to pant and sweat.

No. There was no escape.

The rider lifted himself onto the saddle and the groom unfastened the tether. The beast stood.

A burst of energy! It bucked. It was running, circling… running, circling… running, circling… over and over. But it couldn't escape.

"See the lather?" Lucien said. "The widening nostrils? He's tiring."

More running. Pounding hooves. Running, circling… no escape.

"He's exhausting himself. It's either drop-and-die time or acceptance. He's spent. Drop-and-die or accept."

The animal was now at the point of exhaustion. It stood.

It accepted.

Another man entered the ring and approached the horse's lathered body. He stroked its very wet neck, took a treat from his pocket, and held it to the horse.

"See, Darius?" said Lucien. "Sometimes in acceptance, there is a reward. It's a choice—either to drop-and-die or accept. Even a horse makes choices, and these choices do have consequences. Sometimes there is a reward, for a correct choice. Sometimes there is peace."

The Rabbi spoke again. "Lucien was an excellent tutor. You are at the same point now as that horse, Darius. My friend, the decision is yours: rail or accept. It's all about choices."

I remained silent.

"You have the virtue of hope within you. So many times you could have given up. You had access to drugs, but you also have hope. So many times you could have ended your life, as Balzack planned to do. Your choice to intervene saved not just his life but so many others; like a spider's web, each choice, each consequence, widens its reach. Everything is connected. You have hope, Darius, a great virtue. You have charity also. You stopped to help that woman, the one who touched the hem of my robe. You could have walked on, since your order was to follow me, but you stayed and supported her. You walked with her as her strength returned. And you could have taken coins for writing those letters at the barracks. You could have bought a treat for yourself at the market. But you knew those soldiers are hardly well paid. You even stopped to pick up Simi that day, knowing how attached Little Simon was to his pet. You have the virtue of charity."

Now I did speak, once again letting my mouth outpace my brain. "I was only doing what was logical."

"Really? My mother was so right—you are like the oyster, the hard shell protecting the inner self." The Rabbi's voice grew faint, almost as though he were going "away." But he continued. "The consequences of a choice extend from the present into the future. You know your fear of illness? Someday—not soon, but someday—it will be possible to see the invisible, to recognize what causes sickness. Someday men will see clearly not only the cosmos but travel to the moon and beyond. It will be possible to discover why your hair is a certain colour, and even where your progenitors once lived. Will man one day look in awe and admiration at the Architect and Sustainer? Or will man see himself as the man-god?"

Although he had seemed momentarily distant, the Rabbi suddenly snapped back to me.

"It starts with one act of kindness, Darius. One simple act of kindness. From there, so many interconnections grow. That is why charity is perhaps the greatest virtue. Charity is in you. But you are struggling with the virtue of faith, of acceptance. I understand this isn't easy for one with a brain such as yours. You need time to form a hypothesis, to assay, assess, analyze, deduce, and reach a conclusion. Take all the time you need."

He fell quiet for a moment. I didn't know what to say.

"Best get back before the centurion sends out a search party." The Rabbi laughed "Lucien was right. He says that he often thought you, with such a large brain, couldn't find your way out of a grain sack. Well, you turned left instead of right five alleys back. Shalom."

As I retraced my steps, I realized that the Rabbi had vanished. There was no sign of him anywhere.

I was not at peace.

"The kid's dog okay?" the optio asked when I returned to the barracks.

"It is, sir. Just needed a bit of honey for his throat."

Had I just lied?

I returned to my desk, to the paperwork—the letters, the forms… I returned to sanity. I needed the routine, to focus on what was tangible.

"Darius! Anything to report?"

I looked up at the call of the centurion. His voice was hard to read, as always.

"No, sir," I called back.

I continued with my duties; they usually kept me focused. I needed to focus.

When the workday was over, the soldiers gathered in the dining hall for supper. The centurion hadn't left the office and remained at his desk.

"Darius!"

I ignored my master.

"Darius, are you deaf?"

I went and stood before his desk in the proper position, eyes lowered and head bowed.

"Sir?" I asked.

I expected a reprimand for my tardiness, for having ventured away from the barracks for so long in the middle of the day. I was prepared for the consequences of my actions.

"You are to move into my residence, effective immediately." His words were like a blow to the stomach. "Dismissed."

Why was he ordering me to do this? This would bring much upheaval to my life. But I had been issued an order and I always obeyed orders. Almost always.

The centurion's residence was more than adequate for my needs, it turned out. But the move brought so much change, so very much change. And so much chaos.

Later that evening I heard a knock on the door, followed by the sound of someone entering.

Tobias the house-slave entered. "Do you need anything?" he asked. "Are you settled?"

If my brain weren't so numb and silent, I would have responded, *Settled? I doubt whether I shall ever be settled again.*

Instead I just nodded. Tobias left.

I once again embraced my daily routine. The forms. The letters. The structure. The tangible, where one plus one equalled two. During these work hours, I could focus. But the nights I spent at the centurion's house were just too uncomfortable.

There was a door from my room at the master's house that led to an adjacent garden. The room was becoming suffocating. The silence in my head, smothering. I needed to escape.

Out in the garden, I sat on a bench. At any other time, I would have gone "away," hypothesizing about how a hummingbird's tongue retracts, analyzing which equations had been used in its wing design, wondering whether man could fly; Icarus had a solid plan but had used the wrong adherent…

Today? Nothing. I didn't go "away." I didn't breathe, calm, focus… there was nothing but deafening silence.

"Mind if I join you?"

I turned to find Tobias standing nearby.

It's not my bench, I almost retorted. Instead I kept silent as he sat.

"The master and I…" He didn't seem to know how to begin. "I don't know if you can comprehend this. Have you ever had a friend, Darius?

The master and I are friends. Marcus and I grew up together. My mother was his wet nurse, and then his nanny. I am, like you, slaveborn. Despite the so very great social and status difference between us, we are friends."

Good for you. Now leave me alone.

He rose. "The master wants you to come."

I had been issued an order, so instinctively I followed Tobias to another room in the house where the centurion awaited me. He sat at a table, upon which rested a flask of wine and two cups.

"Sit," my master said.

An order.

Once again I instinctively sat. I obeyed, but I was also silent.

Marcus reached for the flask. "Want some?"

He was asking me whether I wanted to share wine with him? Surely I was going mad. But I had to respond. It sounded like an order...

"No, sir, I am—"

His fist hit the table. "You are so... enough of your slave-speak. You know something! Speak! Say *something*."

An order had been issued, but I said nothing. I sat in the proper position, eyes and head lowered. I didn't know what to say.

"Are you even capable of normal conversation?" the centurion demanded, his voice rising.

Normal? When has my life ever been normal?

"You are so frustrating." He hit the table again. "So very frustrating! Out!"

That order I could obey.

The rest of the week passed the same. My work was a diversion during the day; it was tangible and my duties made sense. At night? The inter-rogations continued. What did the centurion want from me? I always did the forms—always correct and always on time.

"Darius," the centurion called on another night.

When I attended to my master, I found three men in the room. Marcus, Tobias, and the quartermaster Cornelius.

I knew Cornelius, for I had once treated one of his soldiers. I had been assigned to a caravan overseen by Juma, an Egyptian. He had been given a contract to convey Roman cargo, whether human or otherwise, to various posts around the empire. I was being moved from Rome to Fortress Antonia in Jerusalem.

Juma had become aware that I helped the sick and injured and considered my ability to be an asset. And since he was interested in the medical art, he sometimes brought me to markets where I could develop a crate of supplies to be used in healing.

Our caravan stopped unexpectedly one day and Juma and I were summoned to attend to a soldier who had fallen and sustained a serious injury. We had been escorted by a Roman legion for some time, since the trade routes were fraught with bands of marauders.

The centurion of the legion was none other than Cornelius.

"This is your healer?" Cornelius had asked Juma, gesturing to my tunic. "But he's a scribe."

The Egyptian smiled broadly. "Indeed, good sir, but a multitalented one, I assure you."

Cornelius addressed me. "You can help my soldier?"

"I do not know, sir," I humbly replied in my best slave-speech, my head and eyes lowered.

"Juma, you are wasting my time." The centurion turned away in anger.

"Please, centurion, a moment," Juma said. "This man's brilliant mind thinks differently. Darius, explain yourself to the centurion. Look up and tell him why you don't know whether you can be of assistance to the fallen soldier."

I had been issued an order. I had to obey. I always obeyed.

I looked directly at the centurion: "I don't know if I can be of assistance to your soldier, sir, as I haven't examined him to ascertain whether the injury is treatable."

The centurion laughed.

"Brilliant minds," Juma said again. "They think differently."

Cornelius was amused. "Then go ascertain whether you can aid the man."

I had seen many injuries such as this one, and they were difficult but not impossible to fix. The soldier had fallen awkwardly from his horse, landed directly on the shoulder, and separated his arm from its shoulder socket. Painful!

I knelt beside my patient. "I am Darius and have been asked to help you, if you agree."

The man nodded. It was easy to see that he was greatly distressed.

"Allow me to remove your helmet," I said, noticing his sweat and great stress. "And now your robe."

As gently as possible, I began the examination, beginning at the soldier's feet.

One of the stricken man's brothers-in-combat scoffed at me. "You're at the wrong end!"

"Yes, sir," I remarked. "But since your comrade sustained a fall, I must determine whether there are any additional injuries."

This also gave me the opportunity to check the man's pulse points and body temperature.

"All is well, sir," I reported after I had completed my checks. "The shoulder injury is repairable. The procedure will be painful, very painful. But if not done, your arm will be useless. Shall we proceed with the manoeuvre?"

"I am a soldier!" the soldier managed through gritted teeth. "I can bear pain. Fix me!"

I admired his courage. "With your comrade's aid, sir, I shall remove your breastplate."

Once again, this was done as gently as possible. My patient remained stoic throughout the procedure.

"Now, sir, I must cut the seams from your tunic."

Juma handed me a knife. With a little work, I managed to expose the shoulder blade.

"Now, sir, we must work as a team. I mean you no disrespect, but I must straddle you. I will need to exert a great deal of force and leverage. You must follow my instructions."

The man nodded.

"Now, sir, we must both prepare ourselves. This will be difficult. Please follow my directions. We must calm ourselves and focus."

I instructed my patient on how to breathe deeply, to find calm, to focus. I had been trained in these matters. I focused on success; this would be a risky procedure and I had to concentrate on achieving a positive outcome.

"Now, sir, you must focus only on my voice. My words."

I began the procedure. All the while, I told a story.

"When I was but a child, my mentor, a brilliant physician, nick-named me Sponge…" I was using my fingertips to measure angles and distances; I had been trained in this procedure, the specifics of which were akin to physics, algebra, formulae, leverage, and force… "He wished me to absorb all he knew. He believed I had the brain to do so." In my mind, I matched the dislocated bone to its rightful position in the ball joint. "My peers took my nickname as an open invitation to dunk my head into puddles, troughs, and mud pits. They did it so often that I would return to the infirmary totally mired." I prepared myself for the next manoeuvre; it would require all the force I could muster. "My mentor would look at me in disgust and whack…" *Crack!* "…me across the side of the head."

Shoulder and bone were reunited.

It had been Cornelius who added "medically trained" to my list of credentials.

My mind returned to the present, to the interrogation I was having to endure.

Why won't you leave me alone? I wanted to ask, but I stopped myself. Nothing. Silence.

"Sit," my master ordered me again.

And once again I obeyed, taking the proper position.

"We took the blame, you know," Marcus said. "Cornelius and me. Did you think no one would notice? Did you think ever-efficient Rome wouldn't notice what you did? The missing sedation? The omitted words on the sign? You know something, and you will speak or…"

I prepared for a fistfall, for more questioning of my ability to hear, articulate, feel, and otherwise be *normal*.

Cornelius spoke in a soft voice. "Marcus and I are friends."

I don't really care, I almost retorted.

"Actually, the three of us—Marcus, Pontius, myself—are all friends," Cornelius continued. "Our families are longtime allies. We all began our training together. We come from a long line of military men. Marcus, the most efficient one; Pontius, bold and daring; myself, focused on numbers, facts, and strategy."

Are you trying to disarm me? Befriend me so that I divulge information?

I recalled that I'd written many persuasive speeches designed to disarm, charm, and loosen tongues.

But I remained silent.

"I read your reports," Cornelius added. "They were well-written and factual. Many here read them. I remember the one about the girl. Her father came to ask the Rabbi to come to his house. I checked. His name was Jairus. I wanted to verify the story."

The next to speak was Tobias, the house-slave. "I once fell ill, Darius. It was the wasting disease. You are trained, so you know it is incurable. I knew I was dying, I knew I was in the process of dying." He hesitated. "Then I felt my strength returning… and I knew I was cured. I got up and prepared a meal. Marcus hadn't even entered the house."

Marcus leaned forward. "Did you ever wonder why I came that day and asked to see the Rabbi?"

It was not my place, is not my place, to wonder. But I stayed silent. *Did you not see the crowd? Yet you demanded an immediate audience with the Rabbi. Did you not realize how afraid of you these people were? You came in full military uniform!*

Silence.

"I couldn't ask him to come to me." My master's voice sounded distant. "So I went to him. I'd given so many orders and so many had died under my command. But I trusted that if I sought out the Rabbi, he could cure Tobias without seeing or touching him. You reported so many healings… I had no choice but to seek him out. You know something! Speak! Tell me. Tell *us.*"

The anger was rising in Marcus's voice.

I said nothing, but I prepared myself for the thud of his fist hitting the table.

"Darius, there are rumours," said Cornelius. His voice was not unkind. "We need to know if they are true."

I heard many sounds in my head—pounding, pounding, pounding, hoofbeats, pounding, pounding, circling, circling... the groove getting deeper, the track becoming harder... pounding, circling, no escape... circling, running, tiring... so tiring... running, pounding...

"It's drop-and-die time." Lucien! In my head! "See the signs? Heaving flanks, the lather, the redness in the nostrils, the breath sounds... the animal has reached the point of exhaustion. It's drop-and-die time."

"Or acceptance," said the Rabbi. "Even the horse made a choice. It's all about choice. It's your journey. It's your choice."

"The horse is exhausted!" Lucien, again.

Had Lucien been using a metaphor to talk about me? He often spoke in metaphor. Was *I* the one who was spent? Was I circling, looking for escape? But there was no escape! I had to accept... or...

I was so tired. So very tired.

"Look up, Darius!" commanded Lucien. "Read the eyes. It's not all about you. You have patients. You are trained. The eyes... they never lie."

I looked up.

"Put them out of their misery." Now Lucien was yelling at me. "You are trained!

"But this is his journey," said the Rabbi. "Darius must choose."

...eyes of confusion, anger, pain...

The centurion's fist hit the table again. "You know something!"

A softer voice. Cornelius. "Please, Darius, you know the rumours. Are they true?"

So very tired, spent, drop-or-die...

"He lives," I croaked out.

"Finally!" It was Lucien. "Honestly, at times I believed him incapable of finding his way out of a grain sack."

"Such brains as his... they need more time," the Rabbi said. "Shalom, Sparrow."

Peace.

PART THREE
Consequences

I had said the words: "He lives!" But even having spoken the truth, I felt no inner peace; the heaviness remained. Meanwhile, the others in the room continued talking amongst themselves. I heard their voices, but not what they were saying. My thoughts were elsewhere.

I did hear the fist hit the table, though. It startled me.

Breathe, calm, focus.

"You saw him?" Marcus demanded. "The Rabbi?"

"Yes, sir."

"Well?"

I didn't understand. Well, what? What exactly did the centurion want?

Tobias took over. "What did he look like?"

"Like himself."

What do they think he'd look like? I wondered.

"And did he talk?" Tobias asked.

"Yes."

Marcus shook his head in frustration. "Getting anything out of him is…"

"Darius, what did the Rabbi say to you?" said Cornelius. "Was he angry?"

"He was angry with me, but we parted amicably."

The quartermaster hesitated. "Was he angry because… of what we did to him?"

"No, sir. He was angry with me for questioning…" I couldn't go on. I remained silent, my head and eyes lowered, as was proper.

Thankfully, my master dismissed me.

"He's so very annoying," he muttered as I returned to my room.

There was to be a meeting in Caesarea on the Mediterranean coast, where the governor resided most of the year, and all the local centurions were to attend. I was also expected to attend, as the official scribe. I was to go ahead and arrange accommodation for my master and his horse. I would have time to think.

But I didn't want to think, analyze, infer, deduce, or reach a logical conclusion. I was stuck within the conflict between the logical and the illogical. I felt numb and unsettled. Restless.

However, I did reach my destination. Once there, I completed my assignment. Even in mental disquiet, I followed orders.

I had time before the meeting of the centurions, and I needed a diversion. I found myself one afternoon by the horse paddocks. I wondered about these animals. They were so big and powerful, yet they allowed mere humans to control their destinies. Perhaps equine eyes were designed in such a way as to make humans appear bigger, and hence more formidable?

I was "away" and the Rabbi suddenly appeared beside me.

"Darius, I have something for you. It's from little Olivia. She asked me to give it to you." The Rabbi handed me a small wrapped package. "Her parents are potters. They baked and glazed it for her—in admiration, of course."

Was that levity? Yes, he was amused.

I had never received a gift.

"Go ahead," he said. "Unwrap it."

I unwrapped the package to reveal a small sparrow that Olivia had fashioned from clay.

"She was going to make an oyster, but then she decided it would look more like a lumpy stone," the Rabbi added. "And I have messages for you to deliver…"

He went on to describe these important missives I was to convey—

"Darius! Where are you? We have to leave *now*."

My head snapped up at the sound of the centurion's voice. It was filled with anger!

I rushed to his side and together we walked quickly through the maze of rooms. This was a massive walled fortress, much larger than Antonia. Along the way, Marcus was greeted by his peers. They engaged in conversation.

When we arrived at the designated hall, I prepared to begin my notetaking. Many centurions from across the territory under Pilate's control had gathered in this huge space that afforded a view of the sea.

All rose when Pilate entered, and they rose again when the routine meeting concluded sometime later. As I packed up my supplies, I concluded that this would be an easy meeting to summarize.

"Marcus, would you remain?" the governor asked before my master could depart. "I need to go over a few details with you."

The others left, leaving only the three of us behind.

"Come, let's go to a more comfortable room," said Pilate. "Lady Claudia is waiting. Come, Marcus, and your scribe too."

I had to follow. The room we came to was large and full of echoes, and Pilate's wife was waiting for them at a table in its centre. I remained by the door, awaiting instructions.

The three Romans enjoyed refreshments. I surmised they were all well-known to each other, perhaps even friends.

"I laughed in those pesky priests' faces," Pilate was saying. "They told me the Nazarene's followers had attacked the guards and stolen the man's body… preposterous! Roman soldiers are well-armed, seasoned warriors. Can you imagine them running from a mob of fishermen and farmers? The soldiers were punished for leaving their posts, but they must have been spooked. They knew the wrath I'd inflict on them. No, something happened…" Pilate's gaze turned to me, still hovering near the door. "I believe your scribe knows something. He's the one I want to interrogate."

Marcus motioned for me to come forward. "This scribe has always been terse, but recently he has become almost mute. I believe he has experienced something extraordinary but is reluctant to speak of it, even when commanded to do so."

I felt Pilate's gaze on me like an eagle's talons at my throat.

"You know who I am, scribe?" Pilate's manner was imperial.

Breathe, calm, focus,

"Yes, Dominus," I replied.

"Speak to me of this presumed encounter with the one who was crucified."

I could not gather any words to speak to this man so far above my station. I literally couldn't speak.

"You defy me, slave?" Pilate asked harshly.

That word—*slave*—reduced me to my lowest form, stripped me of what little status I held. That word eviscerated me.

Please, Rabbi, I prayed. *This encounter is above my station. I am not trained. Why me?*

In return, I heard his response in my head, his voice perfectly audible: *"You chose this journey, my friend. I warned you it wouldn't always be easy."*

"If your tongue is useless, I can and will order it removed!" Pilate demanded. But then his voice changed, taunting me. "Shall we start anew? Are you certain the Nazarene was dead? You declared deceased all of the crucified men that day."

"Yes, sir," I said. "The soldier's spear did its work. The blood's composition changed, as it does after death. I am trained." *Breathe, calm, focus.* "The Nazarene was dead."

Pilate's voice remained cold, hard, and demanding. "Which brings us right back to you, scribe. Did you see the one known as the Rabbi after his execution?"

"Yes, sir."

"And?"

I was confused. And what? He had asked the question; I had answered it.

"Darius!" My master sounded angry.

"Gentlemen, you know nothing of the art of conversation," said Claudia, the governor's wife. "Honestly! You can't just order someone to speak. Come, Darius, come sit here." She smiled in a friendly manner and indicated the seat next to her. "Or do I have to order you?"

I approached her and sat with my head and eyes lowered. I needed to be calm, to focus. This was going to be a strange encounter.

"Look up," she said, sounding almost amused. "Remember? I like to look people in the eyes. It's okay."

I looked up.

"That's better. Now tell me, how many times have you seen the risen Rabbi?"

"Twice, my lady."

"Twice!?" Marcus said. "When—"

"Marcus, please." Claudia silenced him. "Tell me about the first time, Darius. Where were you? How did the Rabbi greet you? How did you feel? Did he have anything in particular to say to you?"

"I was returning to the barracks when I got lost. The Rabbi was there. He looked and sounded like the Rabbi. He ordered me, in levity, to sit. I overstepped my station. He chastised me. We parted amicably."

"Why did he chastise you?" Claudia was not demanding; she was curious. "Was he angry about his execution?"

"No, my lady. He was angry with me for questioning why his Father had failed to intervene. This was illogical. He explained that his death had been part of his journey, his mission, and one he freely accepted—to die, to redeem, and to rise. I failed to understand him."

Claudia thankfully moved on. "And the second encounter? Tell me about this meeting."

"It happened today, my lady. By the horse paddocks. I was waiting for my master. I was watching the horses. Then the Rabbi was beside me. He had something to give me."

"He gave you something? May I see it?"

"It was something a child made for me, my lady."

I removed the package from my shoulder bag and unwrapped the sculpted figurine of the sparrow. I gave it to her.

"Why it's a little bird!" Claudia said admiringly. "So well crafted. How old is this child? I thought Jewish people never made such objects."

"The child is perhaps eight years old, my lady. A girl. It was made in admiration, not adoration—which means it's not idolatry. The child and I... we have a connection.

"It is lovely." Claudia handed the piece back to me and I returned it to my bag. "Did the Rabbi say anything? Did he merely want to deliver this gift?"

"Yes, my lady. He did ask something of me—something I must do." Now I was becoming nervous. I was not brave. "I have... I have a message for my master. And for you, my lady."

I lowered my head and eyes. I needed time to regroup. I always, almost always, followed orders. But to *give* an order—and to those well above my station?

"The Rabbi has a message for Marcus? For me?" Claudia sounded excited. "How wonderful! What is it? Go on, Darius, please."

"The Rabbi requests that I bring the two of you to him." I had said it. I had delivered the message.

"When? Where?" Claudia turned to her husband. "Oh, Ponti, the Rabbi wants to see me! And Marcus, too."

"Yes, my dear, but this is so sudden," said Pilate, far less animated than his wife. "I need to know more. If I agree, troops must be arranged, a caravan organized. Just where and when is this to happen? Plans must be made, precautions taken."

"When and where is this to take place, Darius?" Claudia asked eagerly.

"We would need to reach the rendezvous spot within the week, my lady, but only I am to know the location," I said. "The Rabbi said that only the three of us are to come."

I tried to sound factual yet humble, a very difficult combination!

"You expect me to allow my wife to go to an undisclosed place to meet a previously dead convicted criminal, accompanied only by a slave?" Pilate demanded with anger in his eyes. He looked at me like I was insane. "Without a cohort to protect her?"

Breathe, calm, focus.

I was not brave, but I had been given an order by him, the Rabbi-risen. I had to obey.

Drawing a breath, I looked up at the governor and made direct eye contact, as though we were equals.

"Sir, with all due respect, I am relaying a message. It is not my request; it is his. As to the secrecy, you must appreciate how terrified his followers are. They are farmers and fishermen. There are some women and children. The secrecy is to protect them, not to put your lady in danger. But it is your decision. I am only the messenger."

I surprised myself with my forwardness, but I immediately lowered my head and eyes, as was proper.

"Please, Ponti, there must be some middle ground here," Claudia broke in. "This means so much to me, to us, to meet this Rabbi, if he is indeed risen. Is there a town nearby, Darius? Perhaps we can travel there, properly equipped, and then the three of us proceed alone to the rendezvous. Marcus will protect me. If we are gone for an unusual length of time, the soldiers can come looking for us. Would that work, my dear? Is that a sensible plan?

Pilate seemed to consider this. "Well, I—"

"If you don't agree, I'll tell my father... and the old goat will order you." Lady Claudia said this in a teasing way. She smiled at him.

I was stunned. The Lady Claudia. Was she truly the emperor's daughter?

"Marcus, what do you think?" Pilate asked. "Is he trustworthy? Do you believe him?"

My master's reply surprised me. I had been expecting more of his annoyance and exasperation with me.

"I do have great difficulty communicating with this one," Marcus said. "He is different. But yes, he has integrity and I do find him trustworthy. I believe he has had an encounter with the one we crucified. I believe he has been given an order by this 'risen Rabbi.' One thing I am most certain of is that Darius *does* obey orders. I will protect your wife with my life, sir."

Pilate still seemed hesitant. "Well, I have reservations."

"Please, Ponti?" Lady Claudia gave him a big smile, "Or else…"

"You always get your way!" Pilate sounded defeated. "But plans must be made, safeguards."

"Of course, my dear. Of course."

My brain was reeling from the revelation that Claudia wasn't only the governor's wife but also Caesar's kin!

We travelled north to Nazareth, accompanied by a small cohort of armed soldiers. With Tobias having stayed back in Jerusalem, I had extra duties with the centurion. These tasks were easy, and once shown I found them easy to remember: armour on and off, boots laced and unlaced… yes, they were easy tasks.

But I feared any conversation beyond "Yes, sir; no, sir." I wanted as little communication with my master as possible. Words, once spoken, could not be edited. I preferred the written word.

I needed to keep my distance. I had always followed, never led. The only time I had ever taken command was in a medical emergency—for that, I was trained. This was different. I was to bring both Marcus and Claudia to the Rabbi-risen. No slave could dare turn his back on a Caesar, and Claudia was of royal blood.

But the Rabbi had given me this order, and I would obey it. I just needed to maintain some distance from them. I needed time to think. I was not brave. I was not a leader.

I thought ahead, looking toward the last leg of the journey, after we'd passed Nazareth and proceeded north from Cana. I was well familiar with the area, for the Rabbi had often sought this place out when he'd needed some personal space from all the crowds that followed him. He'd come here when he needed to relax and regroup.

I knew of two trails to the meeting spot, one very easy and the other harder. The easy trail would be an easy walk for Claudia. Yet the harder route was also the safer one, as it would be more difficult for anyone following us to track. I still didn't fully trust that Pilate would have ordered the soldiers to remain in Cana—and I didn't want to endanger the Rabbi or any of the others.

In the meantime, Claudia was totally enjoying the adventure! She was, of course, riding in a carriage. For her, "camping" was a comfortable enterprise.

On this trip, I suddenly found her to be intimidating in addition to merely confusing.

We were approaching Nazareth near noon when Marcus called to me: "Water my horse." The centurion considered me less his scribe and more his personal slave. Another one of my duties was horse care.

We intended to rest, eat, and then proceed onward to Nazareth where Lady Claudia would spend the night in the local inn.

I led the horse to the river and noticed several other soldiers doing the same. The centurion's horse was thirsty, and I was distracted while it drank. I was mulling over my plan for the rest of the journey when suddenly a fish jumped and the horse shied back from the riverbank.

With a burst of pain, I realized that the beast had landed on my foot! I was in pain but feared the wrath of the centurion were I to let go of the straps.

A soldier standing nearby saw what had just happened and, realizing I was in distress, led his animal over and took charge of my master's horse. An act of kindness.

"Are you okay?" he asked, concerned.

"Perhaps?" I wasn't sure. I let the cool water of the river soothe my foot.

When I pulled it out, I slowly began the examination. I moved my ankle and found it very sore, but I could move it up, down, and sideways. It wasn't broken.

"I'll take centurion's horse," said the soldier. "I'll tether and feed it. You go sit."

"Thank you, sir."

I limped over to a nearby large rock and examined my foot further. I decided it would be best to wear my sandal, lest the foot swell. I suspected two of the toes might be broken, actually. Fortunately the riverbed was soft and had cushioned my foot from more serious damage.

The soldier returned and handed me a stout stick. "I found this. I figured you're going to need it. You're the centurion's scribe, aren't you?"

"Yes, sir, I am. Thank you for your assistance." I appreciated his help; it was so unexpected and, considering the difference in our social status, unnecessary.

I found that I couldn't eat. The pain made me lose my appetite.

As the journey continued, I limped along. Yes, we would definitely be taking the short route!

Nazareth was the Rabbi's true hometown, situated in a hollow formed by the rolling hills of Galilee. We stopped at the inn, knowing that tomorrow we would meet the Rabbi.

I limped into the courtyard. The pain had increased, for the trek had been long. The horses were already stabled; that kind soldier had taken charge of the centurion's mount. I prayed that the Rabbi's Father, Yahweh, would bless this man. He was a soldier with a heart.

I would remain that night in the courtyard with the litter-bearers, as we were slaves. For dinner, food was brought out. Lady Claudia had ordered a rather fine meal. It was placed on a rough-hewn table along with several jars of wine. The litter-bearers were delighted.

Me? Not so much. I remained on the ground with my back against the animal shelter. I had no unction to apply to my wound and I still couldn't fathom eating.

One of the litter-bearers brought me a cup of wine. Why were these people being nice to me?

"Thought you might like some," he said kindly.

I didn't like wine! But I knew I needed to drink something. And perhaps the wine would help me sleep.

"Thank you," I said. "That is very kind of you."

I took a sip. All the while, my foot throbbed.

A servant from the inn soon entered the yard and handed me a small jar. "The domina is concerned you are injured," she said. "She asked that a salve be given. This is what we use on injuries."

I thanked her properly. She was no doubt freeborn.

Claudia confused me. She was so well placed, yet concerned about me? The odd connection between us was baffling. The wine? The salve?

Feeling exhausted, I slept.

Morning brought little relief to my aching foot. Rather than remain inert, I began the day, as usual, with my morning ablutions. When I returned to my bedroll, I found that the litter-bearers had fallen asleep at the table. They were out cold.

The inn's cook saw me when she arrived to remove bread from the outdoor oven.

"Good morning, my lady," I said to her in Aramaic.

Looking confused, she invited me into the kitchen. I planned on inquiring about hot water and I complied.

"Come, sit, have a cup of tea with me," she said. "It gets a bit too quiet in here in the early mornings. I prefer the hustle of the evenings, but Marta is ill, so here I am working an extra shift. You aren't from around here, are you? But you speak Aramaic. Where did you learn our language?"

"I am trained in many languages, my lady. My talent, I suppose."

The friendly cook brought over two teas. "What a wonderful talent to have."

I started to rise, as was proper since she was freeborn, but she was too quick and sat down.

"Without my talent, my lady, the world would be quieter," I remarked. "Without yours, the world would indeed be hungrier."

The cook laughed. "You're with the Romans?"

"Yes, my lady. The centurion is my master."

"Romans! Detestable. Good for nothing." She, like most, had little value for the empire.

"They do build good roads, though, my lady." I had to say something positive. Levity.

Again she laughed. "Not much happens around here, so I suppose it's nice to have this diversion—even if it comes from Romans."

"It's a quiet village, my lady, but it appears to be also quite well-situated." I tried to reciprocate her kindness. "Your village does have an inn."

"Our claim to fame, it seems, is that this is where the one they called the Rabbi grew up. He was executed by the Romans. You've heard of him?"

"Yes, my lady. My centurion is posted to Jerusalem." I didn't want to offer too much information.

"Such a lovely family! Joseph was the carpenter for the area, skilled and always offering a fair price. Mary and I drew water from the same well. She was so pretty, so gentle. She always had a kind word. It really caused a stir when she was found to be with child—and with Joseph away! But he returned, defended her, and married her. A true love story."

We both sipped our tea. My hostess got up and returned with some of the freshly baked bread. She was happy to have company, even a slave's company.

I was curious to hear more about her story. As she spoke, I tried to imagine a young Jesus.

"The family first went to Bethlehem for the Great Census, then to Egypt. I suppose Joseph still had contracts there. They returned five or six years later and we met the boy, Jesus. He was smart, lively, a quick learner, independent, and very popular, but not a fighter—more a peacemaker of sorts. A normal boy. Although my son Samuel once told us that the lads had been out in the hills. Someone took out his slingshot and took down a little bird. Jesus went over and picked up the dead bird, held it, breathed on it… and the sparrow flew away! The boys were astounded! Jesus told them that Yahweh sees value in even sparrows."

Oh, if you only knew…

"When Joseph died, young Jesus took over the business," she continued. "He was skilled like Joseph, good to his mother, and never married. Then, suddenly, he was gone. He returned some months later and rumours spread about him doing some extraordinary things. He was invited to speak and read on the Sabbath, but he scandalized everyone by proclaiming that he was the one foretold by Isaiah, a prophet of old who had written about the Messiah. Jesus was driven out of the temple—the men would've stoned him for such blasphemy, but poof, he was gone. He is Nazareth's only claim to fame. Or infamy? This is where the so-called king of the Jews once lived."

I asked whether the water had heated, as the time had come to attend my master. The cook rose, tended the kettle, and drew a pitcher of heated water.

She seemed concerned as I limped over.

"You're injured," she said.

"It's nothing, my lady. Just a bit of a horse-on-foot incident/"

"I'll get one of the girls to carry up the water. Go and tend to that Roman. Thanks. You're a good listener and helped pass the time quickly. It's otherwise a boring shift."

"My pleasure, my lady. Thanks for your kindness."

I limped up the few stairs, followed shortly by a servant girl. I knocked on the centurion's room.

"Enter," Marcus called. His voice was hard.

The day had begun.

I was still limping when we departed for the short trip to Cana. When we reached the outskirts of the village at midmorning, the cohort of soldiers that had been travelling with us set up camp. I could imagine the alarm this would cause the locals.

At midmorning, Claudia, Marcus, and I proceeded on foot, leaving the soldiers encamped. Marcus had removed most of his military gear but still wore his centurion's tunic, robe, and sword. Physically he reminded everyone exactly who he was. Claudia, however, chose a simple outfit and wore no jewellery, nothing to indicate her high station in life.

As for me, I led the way, limping along. I was familiar with the short, easy trail.

There was a rest stop for Claudia up ahead at the home of a shepherd I knew. I didn't think she was used to this much walking and I certainly looked forward to the break.

"Darius!" called out the shepherd when he saw us on the trail. "The Rabbi said you would be coming—and bringing guests. Welcome!"

I made the introductions. Jonas and his wife Miriam were followers of the Rabbi, and I had tutored their grandson Benjamin. These were simple farm folk. Did they have any idea who Claudia was? I wasn't going to tell them.

"Come. My wife has prepared refreshments." Jonas observed me with concern. "Darius, you're limping. What happened to your foot?"

"It's nothing, sir. A fish, a horse, and a misplaced foot." I tried to sound positive, but it hurt.

"I'm sure Miriam will have something. She's trained." He smiled at his joke.

Miriam was waiting in the yard. Introductions were made all over again, and soon she and Claudia were chatting like old friends. That confused me. Claudia confused me.

We sat in the courtyard as Miriam brought out the meal. We could only eat outside, since all three of us were Gentiles. I had spent years with the Jews and knew their rituals.

I limped over to the well, drew water from an amphora, poured it into a basin, then took a towel from the ledge and hobbled over to Jonas, the head of the household. The grizzled shepherd nodded, washed, and dried his hands.

I moved on to Claudia, the person of next importance.

She was shocked. "Darius, you are a scribe, not a common slave… why are you doing this?"

"Yes, my lady, but Sparrow is wise in our ways," said Miriam. "This act does not demean him. We all know of his superior abilities. The act of humility endears him even more. Darius is our friend, and as a Gentile he has taken this role in our customs."

I felt my face redden as I moved on to Marcus. Then I limped back to the well to undertake my own ablutions. I was obsessive.

The scene struck me as bizarre: three Gentiles, one slaveborn, one a Roman centurion, and the other a daughter of the emperor. Together we sat outside a humble farmer's home, sharing bread with an elderly Jewish shepherd and his wife. I sat apart from everyone, observing the proper protocol.

The scene was too bizarre. My brain felt numb. I wished my foot was numb!

Miriam insisted on looking at my foot and concurred that my toes were broken. Perhaps two? She left and returned with a small jar; the contents had a rather strong, unfamiliar scent.

Miriam insisted on applying some of the ointment on my foot. "It's good for man and beast."

I definitely felt uncomfortable, but the odd-smelling ointment brought some relief.

When the time came for us to depart, Miriam gave me an unexpected hug! I froze.

"Darius, our grandson has begun preparing for his bar mitzvah," she said. "He is studying with the rabbi in Cana. The rabbi asked who had taught Benji to read with such fluency in Hebrew, since we speak Aramaic. We explained that he had a very good tutor. Thanks, Darius. Benji was so nervous, being a farmer's son and all, but now he's a confident student!"

We began our descent to the tip of the Sea of Galilee. Soon we'd be at the designated spot. As we drew closer, Claudia became more excited. My master? He was a hard one to read.

A boisterous black dog suddenly bounded toward us—Simi! That meant Little Simon must be near. I didn't want the centurion thinking this was a feral dog, though, so I had to speak.

I bent down to give Simi a scratch. "Sir, this is the boy's dog, the one I treated." I tousled the dog's fur. "Good to see you looking so well, little dog."

As predicted, Little Simon and several of the other young ones appeared. I was still knelt over, scratching Simi behind his ears.

Soon I felt mistress Olivia's arms around my neck. "The Rabbi said you'd be coming! Did you get my gift?"

"Yes, young mistress. It is beautiful. I shall treasure it always. It's the first gift I've ever received."

Olivia recoiled. "What? You've never received even a birthday present?" Her voice sounded incredulous.

"No, young mistress. That's what makes yours so very special."

Little Simon now recognized the centurion. "Oh! You're Centurion Marcus! I'm sorry I kind of lied, but I needed to get Darius to come." The young master gave me a smile. "I was just following orders." Levity.

How odd; my master smiled! I half-expected his face to crack.

"Have you ever considered a career in the military, young man?" Marcus asked. He now sounded serious.

"No, sir. I'm going to be a fisherman like my dad and kin."

That's when Olivia remembered her manners and curtsied before Claudia. "Mary, the Rabbi's mother, is expecting you, my lady."

We approached the camp and saw several tents, fires, and children playing. Many of the men were out on the water in boats.

"Darius, you made it!" said the Rabbi, smiling broadly as he approached from one of the fires. "Too bad about that foot. Good thing you took the short route. That must hurt."

I made the introductions. Both Claudia and the centurion were speechless. It was indeed the Rabbi-risen!

"Olivia, would you please take Lady Claudia to my mother?" the Rabbi asked.

Olivia would never be tall, but she had confidence. "Yes, Rabbi. Come, Lady Claudia."

"Marcus, come with me. Let's talk." Rabbi and a very shocked centurion walked toward the beach.

I found a place to sit, apart from the others, since they were both freeborn and Jewish. As for my foot, it ached.

When Mary Magdelene unexpectedly appeared, I started to rise, as was only proper.

"Sit, Darius." She laughed. "That's an order! I've brought some refreshments and ointment. The Rabbi said you'd be needing it."

So the Rabbi had known. He always knew. And of course he had known that I would have to choose the easier route, on account of Claudia and my broken toes.

Mary Magdelene sat beside me. "It's okay, Darius."

But I certainly didn't feel okay.

"In a way, we are both outsiders." Her voice sounded wistful. "I'm not slaveborn, but I was a disappointment to my family. I dishonoured them. I shamed them. I wanted more than the life they had. I didn't merely want to become the wife of a Jewish husband. Rising before dawn to grind flour and bake bread? No. I wanted more... nice clothes, jewellery, and a grand house. Sorry, but I wanted slaves to tend to my every need. I wanted *more*. So I sold myself. I had so many lovers—if you can call what I engaged in 'love.' I did amass wealth, though. I invested wisely. I am quite rich.

"I thought that I didn't care if I was shunned by my people—that is, until I met the Rabbi. He was... no, he *is* so very different from any other man I've encountered. So very different. A teacher. A healer. And now, most definitely, he is Yahweh's son-come-to-earth. He welcomed me and saw something in me, something worthwhile. Others were shocked, even stunned, by how he treated me. Those hypocrites criticized the Rabbi, but he explained that a physician doesn't treat the healthy. He cures the sick.

"I was sick inside and He healed me. His mother welcomed me. So you see, Darius, both of us are outsiders. You are obviously a Gentile and lowborn, but I'm a former prostitute and a Jewess. Why have we been brought into this? I don't know, but my soul is grateful. It's extraordinary, yet both of us are part of the Rabbi's band. How are you dealing with everything? Has that brain of yours reached a logical conclusion?"

The beautiful Mary smiled in levity.

"Not yet, my lady," I said. "My brain appears to be stalled."

Obviously she was thinking with her heart. My logical brain kept struggling to make sense of all that had transpired.

"Perhaps this will ease the pain." Mary held out a jar of unction. "Yes, my presence has caused much scandal amongst the Jewish community. So we have something in common."

I looked up and saw the Rabbi and Marcus returning. I couldn't read the expression on the centurion's face.

That evening, the men started a fire burning on the beach. It was time for the small community to gather. I sat on the periphery.

The Rabbi raised his eyes to Yahweh, as he always did, and took a piece of bread. "This is my body…"

A memory flashed at the sound of these words! I was carried back in time to the day after the Rabbi had fed the multitude—the day when two minus one hadn't equalled one. The people had flocked to him, eager for more free food. Had they questioned how the Rabbi upended the very basis of math and science? No. They'd only wanted food.

The Rabbi's response had shocked, even disgusted them. He'd said that he was the bread of life! Unless they ate his body and drank his blood, they would not have eternal life with his Father Yahweh and the great I Am. "The shepherd knows his flock," he had said.

So this is what the Rabbi meant, I thought. *Of course! Food becomes part of anyone who eats it. The Rabbi wants to be part of us! Me? Perhaps not. I am a slaveborn Gentile…*

Everyone was chatting, eating, and enjoying themselves—they were all freeborn. I was not. They had freedom. I did not. They could choose their destinies. I could not. I had been born to serve.

I was feeling sorry for myself!

Memory once again consumed me. I was travelling with Lucien to a grand villa. But instead of going to the house, we steered toward the stables which were equally as grand. Lucien was to inspect a new horse, a gift for our master's son's birthday.

The horse was music in motion! It had come from Egypt, so unlike the local equines. Small and graceful with an arched neck, full mane, small ears, large expressive eyes, and an unusual dish nose, I took note of its delicate legs. It didn't move, it flowed!

Lucien finished the inspection and pronounced the animal young, fit, and sound.

While we returned home, I was sullen and pouting. I had never received a gift in my life and didn't even know when my birthday was. It just wasn't fair!

Lucien recognized my mood and chided me: "You want a pony?"

"No, sir… it's just—"

"Just what? Just that he's freeborn, rich, and you're not? Well, that's life. It isn't fair! Stop pouting and count what you do have: food, shelter, and the chance to learn a noble profession. Remember that you weren't sold off to some brothel in Rome, or some mine in the territories. Stop moping. We have work to do."

"Yes, sir."

But secretly I wished that the young master would be tossed off that horse—and maybe even stepped on!

We were called back to the estate a few days later. It turns out that the young master had indeed fallen off his new pony. Lucien diagnosed the boy's broken collarbone and tightly bandaged the shoulder to immobilize it.

That's when I realized that not only do actions have consequences, but apparently thoughts as well. I also learned that the beautiful animal was ordered to be destroyed.

On that day, I realized that envy is evil.

My mood did improve during our visit with the Rabbi and his followers on the Sea of Galilee. Some young ones came by to ask whether I'd play a word game with them. It was one I recognized, as I had devised some simple word games in months past to help the younger ones learn vocabulary in Latin and Greek.

When it was time to retire for the night, as usual I distanced myself from the disciples. Marcus followed my lead; we were both Gentiles.

Feeling unsettled, I stared up at the sky. Far beyond the cosmos lived Yahweh. I suspected the Rabbi would soon be returning to his Father and the great I Am. I imagined the place where the chosen ones would spend eternity, where the sheep of Israel would lay in green pastures, a perfect place for the Shepherd's flock.

I was not part of that flock.

I wondered about Marcus and Claudia. I had been ordered to bring them to the Rabbi. Perhaps some freeborns and nobleborn Gentiles also had some access to Yahweh's eternity? Perhaps they were a different breed of sheep?

Where was my place, all of us who were born slaves? Would I be the servant, the messenger, the drudge? If I was even allowed admittance to Yahweh's kingdom, did an eternity of servitude await me?

Yes, I was very unsettled.

If Lucien were alive, he would have reminded me to count my blessings, but right now that was so very difficult. At least I had obeyed the Rabbi's order and successfully delivered Marcus and Claudia to him. I had been brought into this journey, and I'd chosen to stay.

Now the journey was complete.

Perhaps that's what was upsetting me. I regretted that the journey was ending! Lucien had been correct: he had warned me not to let my heart rule my head. Leaving these people would cause me much sadness.

Simeon-of-the-knife appeared and settled beside me.

"Just like old times, eh, Sparrow?" His voice sounded uncharacteristically cheerful.

"Yes, sir."

"You know, Sparrow, I now realize why the Rabbi gave you the option to tag along with us. I definitely wasn't happy about it, but now I understand." He was silent for several moments. "By the way, the Rabbi has given Big Simon a nickname. He's now called Peter... Cephas. Rock. It suits him. My real name is also Simon, of course. That's why we decided to add an *e* to my name... to avoid confusion."

Whether Simon or Simeon, you would gladly slit my throat. And now I've brought a centurion and the emperor's daughter into the group!

I said nothing.

A few moments later, the centurion spoke.

"May I ask why everyone refers to Darius as Sparrow?" Marcus asked the other man.

"Look at him," said Simeon-of-the-knife. "Between you and me, you're a hawk. Hawks devour sparrows. I'm a pigeon. We chase sparrows away from the seeds. Darius is caught in the middle. He must always be vigilant. He must weigh all he says and does carefully in order to survive. He's a sparrow. Although the Rabbi's mother once said that he was more an oyster—such a hard shell." He chuckled but then grew very serious. "You know, if Simon Peter hadn't been there, I would have killed you the first time we met. I would have slit your throat. Now I know how wrong I was, how wrong I have been. I was consumed with my own self-righteousness. I refused to recognize what the Rabbi saw in you.

"Remember the first day when Little Simon's pup hackled and ran toward me? I now realize that the dog wasn't protecting Simon from me. It was protecting you! Even a small puppy sensed what the Rabbi saw in you. I only saw what you weren't: Jewish.

"I watched you with the children. I monitored you, suspecting that you'd throw in something anti-Jewish or pro-Roman. You never did. The children loved you. Even the teens and moms would stand near listening to you interact with the children. They heard the joy in your voice. I only saw that you weren't one of us. I was so blinded by my own ego. I continued to see you as an object, a threat that needed to be destroyed before you defiled us. And you weren't even armed! But that was about to change.

"It was Passover Thursday and we were all together. Then the Rabbi did something shocking! He took a basin and towel and began to wash our feet. A slave's job. The Rabbi, Yahweh's own son, doing a slave's job? Peter protested. But Rabbi reproached him, reminding us that our mission is to serve—to bend down, like a slave, and serve others. That's when I realized that you do exactly that. You live a life of service. That's how Jesus expects us to live, serving others. That's why the Rabbi invited you to follow us. He was using you as an example. To think I was so keen on killing you."

My mind was reeling at this speech. "But, sir, the choice to serve is not mine. I was born into servitude."

"That's the point, Sparrow," Simeon-of-the-knife said. "Now we're born into service, feeding the poor and helping the disadvantaged. We are to serve—like you. Remember that actions have consequences. Jesus also taught us that. You always say, 'I simply follow orders,' but the lesson is in *how* you serve, Sparrow. I've never heard you complain, groan, or shirk a duty. You serve the way the Rabbi expects us to serve."

I didn't respond. What could I say?

As usual, I awoke early. The others were sleeping, but I limped away to perform my morning ablutions. By the time I returned, I found the Rabbi sitting and facing east, where the sun had barely risen.

"Come, Darius, sit with me."

I limped over and sat. I always obeyed orders.

"How's the foot? How's your head? There's a lot for you to absorb." Rabbi sounded amused.

"The foot... it's healing. The brain, not so much."

"Go on. Talk to me."

"Sir, I know you are otherborn. Based on all I've witnessed, I can logically conclude that you are indeed the one your people call the Messiah. I know you are Yahweh's son sent to earth. I would so like to read the words of your people's prophets. Their prophecies, I believe, would certainly prove that you are their fulfillment. Of course, I have no access to these; they are for Jewish eyes only."

"Soon I will be returning to my Father's home." Rabbi sounded—thoughtful? pensive? "It's lovely, earth, but it pales compared to the realm where Yahweh resides—"

"But, sir, that's the point." I had spoken without thinking! I let my mouth outpace my brain! "Yahweh's home, where you're going, where your flock is going, where your people are now entitled to enter... it's for your flock, the people of Israel—"

"Darius, when did I ever say that my Father favours only the Israelites?" asked the Rabbi, cutting me off in turn. "Think! Did I heal only Jews? Did I ever ask anyone's ethnic background before healing or talking to them? Remember the Gentile mother who asked that her daughter be cured of a demon? How I enjoyed that encounter! Such a clever woman, retorting that even dogs receive the crumbs from the master's table. What an answer! Did I not cure her child? Did I not die a slave's death? Yes, the Israelites got it into their heads that they enjoy exclusive access to Yahweh and have a monopoly on salvation. Some think that I Am favours only them. But Darius, did I ever preach that? Sparrow, my Father is your Father too, even if the son has yellow hair, a notch in his ear that doesn't hurt, and can transcribe in lots of tongues."

Levity.

The sun was rising and the Rabbi rose. "Time for morning Shema, to praise Yahweh. A nation united in prayer."

I repeated the words regarding the Shema, which I had once said to the Rabbi. It seemed so long ago.

"I am sure Yahweh is well pleased," I added afterward.

"By the way, Darius, I wasn't worried about the fish-horse-foot incident. You are trained, after all." The Rabbi sounded amused. "Lady Claudia isn't accustomed to forced marches."

Once breakfast was eaten and farewells made, it was time for us to retrace our steps before the soldiers began searching the trail for us.

I didn't learn what the Master said to either Marcus or Claudia, and it wasn't my place to ask. But I pondered what the Rabbi had said to me, that his Father is my Father, too.

The three of us walked—well, I limped—down the trail in silence.

When we got to the home of Jonas and Miriam, the shepherd's wife had prepared lunch for us. Again we sat outside in their courtyard. She asked about my foot and I assured her that it was healing, that Mary Magdelene had provided me with a jar of salve.

"And I am well trained," I added for levity.

Before our departure, Claudia gave something to Miriam, something I couldn't see. Miriam protested, but the governor's wife insisted.

"It's for your grandson," said Claudia. "This rite of passage warrants a fine celebration."

The walk back to Cana was easy; it was, after all, the easy trail.

"Couldn't it have been a couple of wasp stings?" I muttered to myself about my injury. "Why broken toes?"

After we entered the encampment where the cohort had been waiting, the kind soldier sought me out to ask how my foot was.

"Are you the scribe?" he asked "The one who spent time with him— the Rabbi?"

I had to respond, for he had asked a question and I felt I owed him something for his kindness. "Yes, sir, I am."

"Did he really do the things you reported?"

I was a bit unnerved by this. How many had read my words? I had assumed that some bureaucrat would glance over my writings and file them along with piles of other documents. Rome loved paperwork.

"Yes, sir, the Rabbi did the things I reported," I replied, trying to sound factual. "I am a good scribe. I did exactly as I was ordered."

The soldier seemed amazed. "What an experience!"

"It was indeed, sir." I used proper slave speak, since I wanted the conversation to end.

For the first time in a long while, I was actually happy to hear Marcus's call interrupt us: "Darius, where are you? Come!"

I limped away. "Coming, sir."

Soon the camp was dismantled and we moved on to Nazareth, Marcus in full uniform and Claudia in her carriage. As we travelled, I thought about the Rabbi's words about life being akin to a journey. I feared where my journey was headed. Logic concluded that there would be changes ahead.

We were again to spend the night at the inn in Nazareth, and again the "grand lady" ordered a fine meal to be served to her litter-bearers out in the courtyard.

But not for me. Instead the inn's servant girl told me that I was to follow her to Claudia's chambers.

The rooms prepared for Claudia were adequate. She and Marcus sat at the table, and there was a place for a third. I stood by the door as was proper, my head and eyes lowered, wishing to be out in the courtyard and dreading the order I knew was coming.

Breathe, calm, focus.

"Come, Darius, join us," said Claudia. "Sit. We need to talk."

I had to obey. It was an order.

Claudia took the liberty of serving up the meal as Marcus poured the wine. My brain—and stomach—reeled. I couldn't possibly eat with them! They were well above my station. How I wished I were out in the courtyard.

"Do I have to order you to eat?" Claudia sounded amused.

"Thank you, my lady." I tried to sound humble yet grateful. "I am content."

"I very much doubt any of us is content," the centurion said. "First of all, you're under protective custody from now on. You're confined to the barracks. I shall select men I can trust to guard you at all times."

Me, guarded? Grounded? Confined to the barracks? What had I done? I had only been following orders!

I remained silent.

"Darius, look up," Claudia said gently. "You are in danger. All of the Rabbi's followers are. There are eleven apostles and many, many more disciples and followers to carry on spreading the Rabbi's message. You, however, are the only Gentile who has witnessed much of what he said and did. Many have read your reports. The Rabbi's enemies, not to mention the hierarchy of his own people, will seek to silence anyone connected to him. He warned us of this. We cannot protect the eleven, or the others. We can and must protect you. You are the only non-Jewish witness."

I couldn't respond. I was in shock.

"At some point you'll be transferred to Caesarea," Claudia said. "Not immediately, as that would arouse suspicion. There are spies everywhere. In the meantime, you'll continue your duties under Marcus with the restrictions. I will arrange a position for you in Caesarea, perhaps as my personal secretary. But first I'll have to get Pontius to promote my present one. We must do this discreetly. Eventually, when things cool down, we can begin working with Mother Mary and Mary Magdelene to establish a safehouse for widows and orphans. The plan is so exciting—to feed, shelter, clothe, help, and teach the ones most in need. It will be just like he taught!"

The centurion was more pragmatic. "But first, my lady, we must enact the safety protocols."

"Of course, Marcus. I leave those in your capable hands. Now let's eat. I'm ravenous."

I was not! As I had feared, my life was indeed in flux. Everything was about to change. I needed structure and stability. And now I had a new fear. Was my life truly in danger? I was not brave.

My master's voice pulled me back to the present. "You'll stay in the next room tonight, with me."

"Sir, would that not draw more suspicion?" I asked in my best slave-speak. "Surely there is little danger this far from Jerusalem."

I didn't want to stay inside the inn.

Thankfully, the centurion concurred. "Agreed."

"Now eat, Darius," said Claudia being very motherly; she was very confusing. "Even a bit."

The servant girl came in to remove the dishes. "Shall I take him back to the courtyard?" she asked.

"That won't be necessary," said Marcus. "I'm going to check on my horse; she seemed a little off on the journey. I'll escort Darius."

My master wasn't taking any chances. He was serious. Indeed, my life had been upended.

"Look who's back?" one of the litter-bearers joked when I got back to the courtyard. "Enjoy your evening with royalty?"

"No, sir. It's just that the lady is without her personal scribe. And I am trained." I tried to sound convincing without actually telling a lie.

It was a starry night, a quiet night, and I found myself praying.

Yahweh, Your son told me You are the Father of us all. It was an honour and a privilege to have shared but a bit of his journey. I am now told that perhaps through this association my life may be in danger. I do not fear death. It's either the ending or, as your son taught, the beginning. Am I allowed to ask, if I am to die, that it be a quick death? I am not brave. I fear his enemies may try to coerce the names of his followers from me. I am not brave. And please protect the children. Keep them safe. The Rabbi once told me that the journey wouldn't always be easy. I understand this. But I am not brave. If death, please make it a quick one.

I quickly added, *Thank You, sir,* remembering how disappointed the Rabbi had been when the lepers hadn't expressed gratitude.

I was a light sleeper, perhaps because of all the interrupted sleeps of my childhood. I recalled the night terrors of contagions, or those moments when Lucien had awakened me to say that illness happens day and night—

I heard a noise, saw a blade coming at me, and thanked Yahweh that at least my death would be quick.

But then the knife dropped. And a moment later, so did the body of my unseen assailant. My master had posted a guard, who had protected me.

"Are you okay?" the soldier asked.

"Yes, sir. Thank you."

"Is he dead?"

I felt my attacker's body, searching for a pulse point. I encountered wet blood and realized he was unconscious.

"He's alive," I concluded, at last finding the man's pulse. "We need to move him. Get light, water, towels. I'm trained."

"You're going to fix him? He tried to kill you."

"Life is funny that way."

As Lucien would have told me, *"Healers aren't judges. Get on with it!"*

The litter bearers were awake now.

"What's going on?" one of them asked.

"This gentleman seems to have an aversion to yellow-haired people," I said, trying levity. "This kind soldier intervened. Would you help move him to the table?"

The litter-bearer balked. "What are you going to do?"

"I'm going to clean and dress the wound."

"Thought you were a scribe."

"I am. I'm also trained in medicine."

"He tried to kill you!"

"Yet I'm the one who's going to mend the wound. Life is funny."

The man narrowed his eyes at me. "You're odd!"

"Yes, I've been told that many times."

The litter-bearers moved my assailant just as he was regaining consciousness. The soldier then returned with a servant girl and some of the items I'd requested.

Now that I had light, I began the examination. It was a clean cut to the shoulder and appeared to be through and through. No major blood vessel damaged. He was a lucky man. This was all fixable.

Marcus appeared in the courtyard. "You okay?" he asked, sounding concerned.

"I am, sir, thanks to this soldier."

"What are you doing?" the centurion asked.

"I'm going to clean and bind the wound."

"Why? He tried to kill you!"

"One of life's ironies, sir."

The inn was now astir. I asked for linen, more water—in separate basins please—and sour wine. The physician in me took command. I began cleaning the wound.

Claudia was the next to appear. The same questions, the same answers. I bound the wound tightly, unable to do more. I now needed to wash the blood from my hands! I was obsessive.

The centurion began questioning the man. He learned that someone had given him money to kill the yellow-haired scribe staying at this inn. The man hadn't known his employer; he had just needed the money.

"You tried to destroy imperial property," said Claudia. "That's punishable by crucifixion."

Both my assailant and I cringed at the sound of that word.

"My lady, may I speak?" I had to be brave. It was above my station to interfere.

Breathe, calm, focus.

Claudia appeared shocked, but she replied, "Yes, Darius, of course."

"I'm fine. This man is repaired. There's no real damage done. Could he not just be let go?" I tried levity. "I doubt there are many yellow-haired slaves around for him to seek out. He's learned a lesson. All's well."

The truth was that I didn't want to be haunted by yet another death.

"Why, Darius?" she asked. "There are laws. Justice. Order to be maintained. Actions have consequences, you know that." Claudia was, after all, the governor's wife; law and order was in her blood.

"A very wise man once said, 'Go and sin no more.'"

Claudia turned to the centurion. "Marcus, what do you think?"

"Get out of here!" Marcus said to the assailant. "If I ever see you near any one of my soldiers or slaves, I will personally string you up!"

The man fled.

Shortly after he'd gone, a servant girl appeared in the courtyard. "The cook has made you a cup of sweet tea, my lady."

"Give it to Darius." Claudia smiled. "He's had a rough start to the day."

It *had* been a rough start to the day!

"Thank you, my lady," I said. "In this case, I do accept."

We began the journey back to Caesarea, Claudia in her carriage, Marcus leading his troops, and me limping behind, my head aching from lack of sleep.

I imagined the Rabbi; he would be amused by all this. He had warned me that the journey wouldn't always be easy.

Claudia's return to Caesarea was cause for a joyous celebration. Fortunately, my presence was not requested. I needed space and quiet. I needed sleep!

The centurion and I set out for Jerusalem the next morning. I still limped, but the pain had eased. Once again I wished that I had suffered no worse than a couple of bee stings.

My master had to keep circling his horse to stay close to me.

"You need a horse," said the centurion, exasperated.

We stopped for lunch, removing some food that the kitchen in Caesarea had provided for us. Marcus took a big drink from his wineskin and promptly spit out the contents.

"Tea! Who puts tea in a wineskin?"

I tried hard to stifle a laugh. "Perhaps you have mine, sir?"

"Disgusting!" He was not amused. "You don't eat much."

Why would he care, or even notice? Was he trying to initiate a dialogue?

"Enough, sir," I said, hoping to end the conversation. Words could be dangerous.

"I really am trying to understand you, to be patient… but you are so…" The centurion cut off his own words. "Where did you come from?"

Yes, the centurion was definitely trying to engage in conversation.

"Rome, sir," I answered in my best slave-speak.

"I know that!" He sounded both frustrated and angry. "Before that, though? Perhaps understanding you will help me be less annoyed with you. I fear we'll be spending a lot more time together. I don't always want to be banging my fist on a table every time I need to get you to speak."

Was that levity?

"Tuscany, sir."

"Where did you learn so many languages? Your medical training?"

"Tuscany, sir."

"You are positively, frustratingly, annoying!"

Even without his fist hitting a table, I flinched.

The centurion took a deep breath and softened his tone. "Darius, have you ever been beaten?"

"Yes, sir, in Tuscany." I prayed this questioning would end. I didn't want to go there. I had put the past where it belonged—in the past.

He asked no more and we resumed our journey.

When we arrived in Jerusalem, a stack of papers awaited me. I was glad, for I needed the work. Words and numbers calmed me and kept me sane.

The optio greeted my master cordially. "Didn't expect you to be gone for so long, Marcus. Rumour has it you and Lady Claudia were off on some kind of adventure."

"Yes. The domina decided it would be 'fun' to explore the local terrain, to see how the locals live… that sort of thing. She's not at all like her father."

"Thank goodness!" retorted the optio. "But why you, sir?"

"Because of him." The centurion shrugged at me.

I was already in the process of clearing some of the paperwork that had accumulated on my desk. I was a good scribe.

"Lady Claudia took a liking to your scribe?" Apparently the optio found this amusing. "Must be his colouring."

"It's his fluency in the local tongue, and his knowledge of the area," said Marcus. "She insisted on visiting a typical shepherd's dwelling. Darius knew of one. We ate outside in the courtyard. The house? A hovel! Lady Claudia ate peasants' food!" He sounded disgusted.

The optio found this even more amusing!

I at least had my work. The day passed quickly. These mundane duties also kept fear away. I was not brave.

"Darius," my master called as evening came around.

I had to respond. "Sir?"

"Come."

I had to obey, for an order had been given.

Breathe, calm, focus.

"You'll be staying the evenings at my residence," the centurion said. "It will be safer there. To avoid suspicion, I'll say you are to tutor Tobias, teaching him Hebrew. Get ready. I want to leave soon."

Tobias was surprised to see me. That didn't surprise me, of course. The centurion explained the situation, adding that to everyone else I was to be known as his Hebrew tutor, there to help him shop at the market stalls more efficiently.

"Aramaic, sir. The vendors speak Aramaic. Hebrew is spoken by the elite, as well as in temples and synagogues."

I had spoken out of turn! I'd let my mouth precede my brain! Both my master and Tobias stared at me.

"Sorry, sir, I let my mouth—"

"The sparrow speaks!" Marcus found this amusing.

While on base, at work, I was confined to my cell due to my "spurious" behaviour in Caesarea. Indeed, my journey had altered.

One day when there was a disturbance in the city, all the troops were on high alert. Jerusalem was packed with merchants and tourists from afar. Somehow the crisis seemed to involve the Rabbi's apostles and disciples.

Yahweh, protect them, I prayed. *And the children, watch over them. Thank You.*

I moved papers around. I was worried.

Later that evening, the centurion explained what had happened. There had been no uprising, but something most unusual had occurred. The Rabbi's followers had begun telling anyone who'd listen about Jesus, his teachings, his death, and his resurrection. The unusual part was that no matter what part of the empire those assembled came from, no matter their native tongue, the language barrier was broken! This amazed everyone! Many who had heard about or seen the Rabbi over the years came to a fuller understanding. There were many more believers afterward.

This was good, yes, but also dangerous. The leaders at the temple were very much a presence in the city.

A few days later, the centurion was out of the office, having left the optio in charge. I was at my desk.

That's when the temple leaders entered. I recognized them, which wasn't hard to do, given that their clothing was so elaborate. Yes, these were chief priests.

The optio did not rise. He merely asked, "Can I help you?"

"We wish to borrow the services of your scribe, the one called Darius," spoke one who had a honeyed tongue. He was so innocent, so cordial. "He is proficient, we have heard, in many tongues and we require his services in translating a document."

The optio was unimpressed. "You have your own people. Use them."

"But, sir, you don't understand—"

"I understand that you are on imperial grounds. You have no authority here. Leave or I'll have you escorted out."

"Sir, this is so irregular."

"Out!" Now the optio stood in all his imperial glory.

Indeed, all of us who followed the Rabbi were in danger. The Jewish authorities had silenced the Rabbi and failed. Now they would silence his followers.

I was protected, but I feared for the others; I feared for the children.

I was out in the garden. My mind was "away."

Suddenly I realized that Tobias was beside me. I startled.

"Marcus wants you to come, but first he asked me to explain," the house-slave said. "He has, you know, difficulty communicating with you. The three of us are going out tonight, to a small gathering of the Rabbi's Gentile followers. Many have read your reports. Many want to learn more about him. You will be asked about what you witnessed, what he taught. Marcus, as always, has a plan. This will be done slowly, in stages, not all at once. Don't worry. All will be fine."

But I was worried. Why me? I was not brave. This was above my station. I wanted to stay in the solitude of the garden. I wanted to be "away."

I could not. I didn't control my own movements. My master did. I was slaveborn. I belonged to the emperor.

At the meeting, there were perhaps a dozen people assembled, all free-born—and judging from the area of town we were in, all were very wealthy and important. I kept my eyes and head lowered as I repeated my mantra.

Breathe, calm, focus.

"Sit, Darius," Tobias said, sitting beside me. "It'll be fine. Don't worry. Remember when Marcus said, 'the sparrow speaks'?"

If I had been a sparrow, I'd have flown away.

The centurion knew these people. They were his peers. He began welcoming them and explaining the difficulty he had with me when it came to communication.

"Darius is an excellent scribe. He is fluent in many languages, one of the reasons he was chosen for this assignment. Rome was naturally concerned as the fame of Jesus of Nazareth increased and crowd size grew. You've read his reports. Darius may not be, shall I say, a conversationalist, but he has integrity and always completes assignments accurately. I trust his honesty. However, please don't be alarmed; to get this one to say more than "Yes, sir" or "No, sir," I may have to issue rather emphatic orders."

Levity?

He turned to me. "Darius, I order you to tell us about your first encounter with the Rabbi!"

I didn't want to respond, but an order had been issued.

Lucien was suddenly in my head. *"Remember your first operation— the amputation? You asked, 'Why me?' and I responded, 'Because you're ready. Now move!'"*

"The Rabbi found me amusing," I said at last, answering Marcus's question. I explained the circumstances that had brought me before him, about meeting his mother, sitting around the campfire, and being given a choice. "Yes, he found me amusing, but he added that if I chose to follow him I must move closer to the fire, lest the hyenas get me."

As a Gentile, I explained, I had never entered a Jewish home, never mind the temple. Definitely I had never stepped into a synagogue. I could only attest to what I witnessed outside these institutions: the blind seeing, deaf ears opened, and lepers cured. Most astonishing of all, I spoke of seeing two people, a teenager and the Rabbi's friend Lazarus, rise from the dead.

"Just to be clear," someone spoke up. "You are a physician?"

I gulped, having feared that a person would eventually ask this. It was a logical question.

"Yes, sir, I am," I replied. "My training began when I was a child. I learned under a skilled physician in Tuscany. It continued in Alexandria where I studied for five years."

Having anticipated that I would be asked about my qualifications, I withdrew a document from my shoulder bag. The document was issued in my name. It confirmed that I had successfully completed my training and graduated from Isis Medica, the school of medicine in Alexandria. My oath had been taken in absentia.

"Yes, I am a qualified physician." I passed the document to my master. "The Rabbi never asked about my qualifications, but he knew. I was his witness. I am trained. I am fully qualified. What I witnessed? Everything is very true."

"Darius, why did I not know about this?" Marcus demanded. He sounded upset. "I was told you were a scribe with some medical training."

"No one ever asked, sir," I responded in my best slave-speak, head and eyes lowered. I waited for the centurion's fist to hit the table.

Someone changed the direction of the conversation, a woman who was curious about the Rabbi's mother. What could I share about her?

"She unnerved me," I said. "She still unnerves me, my lady, even to this day."

The lady pressed on. "And what exactly does that mean? I don't understand."

Neither do I, I wanted to say, but I silenced that thought. I had to try to explain.

"I've had no experience with the concept of a mother, as I never knew the one who birthed me. I don't understand that connection, that bond. The first time I saw Mary embrace her son—that connection confused me. It unnerved me. *She* unnerved me. I have no experience in such matters. Mary is, however, remarkable."

I went on to explain about our discussion about being normal versus otherborn, including her encounter with a disembodied spirit, an angel. I also told of her people's commitment to await the coming of a Messiah who would make right all the wrongs—and she was asked to be the mother of this Messiah. I explained her relationship with Joseph, his experience with the angel, and the details of their trip to Bethlehem—the Rabbi's birth, the shepherds, the Magi, the order from Herod, and their eventual escape to Egypt.

"That's enough for the evening," the centurion finally said.

I was relieved to fall silent again as the guests mingled while sharing refreshments. I tried to fade into the background.

Marcus was annoyed with me as we walked back home.

"You could have told me about Alexandria," he said. "You only mentioned Tuscany."

"But, sir, you asked where I originally came from. That was Tuscany." I couldn't understand; he had asked a question, and I had answered.

"Why were you in Alexandria? Who would pay to send someone like you to such a prestigious academy?"

"I wasn't the one sent, sir. That was the master's son. I was to be the young man's house-slave in Alexandria, but he substituted me for himself at the academy. He knew I had the ability to learn, that my brain absorbs knowledge. I took every course available. Medicine was not my preferred course of study—blood, disease, contagion—but my mentor was a brilliant doctor! His plan was for me to follow in his footsteps. I took the classes to honour him. I owed him that."

"Surely the instructors knew the truth about you." Marcus wouldn't let the matter drop. "You hardly look Roman."

"They knew, sir. They told me at the end of my training. But they decided to see what my brain was capable of achieving. The degree I earned was issued in the young master's name. When one of the instructors asked about my real name, I thought he was merely curious. I had no knowledge that this document, confirming my training, even existed—that is, until my master's estate and everything on it became property of the emperor. A lawyer found it among my master's papers and kindly gave it to me." I paused for a few moments. "I intended no disrespect to you, sir. No one ever asked. The past is the past."

My daytime incarceration continued. It was restrictive, but at least I was safe. I worried about the Rabbi's other followers, though.

The evening meetings continued, always at different houses. A few new faces were added over time. These conversations were difficult for me, for the guests broached many topics. Who was the Rabbi? What was his connection with Yahweh and I Am? The only comparison I could offer was heart, brain, and body. The Father, Yahweh, was like the brain; I Am was like the heart; Jesus was the embodiment of God-come-to-earth.

I was not trained in such matters. The Romans had so many deities.

As best I could, I explained the Rabbi's teachings using parables. These were powerful, wealthy Gentiles. What did they know about seeds and planting? Did they understand that a lost sheep would remain frozen in fear, immobilized as the shepherd sought to carry it back to the fold on his shoulders? I could give firsthand testimony as to the Rabbi's death and my encounter with the Rabbi-risen. What more did they want from me?

"Was it the healings, cures, and improbable raising of the dead that convinced you that this Jesus is God's son on the earth?" someone asked.

That I could answer. "No, sir, not the healings. The Rabbi once looked at me with amusement, saying, 'Physicians, what do they know?' We were in Naim. It was the time when the Rabbi raised the widow's son to life after I had pronounced the boy dead. Later, the Rabbi changed a few pieces of bread and fish into an amount ample enough to feed thousands. That's when I accepted who the Rabbi was. Who but a God, the God and creator of the world, had such authority over the basic laws of math and science? Logic dictated that I was in the presence of God on earth."

But they wanted more. The woman who had questioned me about the Rabbi's mother wanted more. She wouldn't give up!

"I'm curious about *you*," the woman said. "To understand and accept him and his message of peace to people of goodwill, I need to understand how you, both a Gentile and a born slave, fit into the picture."

Was she questioning my integrity? Did she think I was somehow benefiting from any of this? I glared at her totally inappropriate question, which was a totally inappropriate thing for me to do.

"Darius!" called the centurion.

I snapped to attention, realizing that I had broken protocol!

"I'm warning you," said Marcus. "You will conduct yourself respectfully. You've been asked and you will answer. We need to know—"

I have never been prone to outbursts, for they are illogical. On this occasion, though, I did the illogical.

"You know what, sir?" I cut him off. "Do you control what I'm thinking? Feeling? Do you also own my thoughts?"

I braced for the inevitable fist fall—or worse. Actions had consequences. Like a petulant child, I wanted to shout, "She started it!" But I remained silent.

It was Tobias who de-escalated the situation.

"We need to know you," he said kindly. "Can you share more than facts and figures? You were part of the inner circle. We're not intruding. We're just asking how *you* feel about all that has happened."

I'd gone this far and resigned myself; at least my upcoming whipping would be worthwhile.

"How do I feel?" I took a deep breath. "To understand *him*, you need to understand *me*? I don't know how it is possible to answer, for I have never been *me*. I've always been what others wanted, what they demanded me to be. Perhaps that's why the Rabbi found me amusing and interesting, as in every possible way I was so very different from his followers. Perhaps that's why he called me a sparrow. I have a brilliant mind; I know that. Perhaps that's why my mentor nicknamed me Sponge as a young boy. I have always been different. Perhaps my brain is all I am. I was content with that. Brains don't feel.

"And of course I can decode and decipher easily. But you want me to describe an emotion? I struggle with feelings. Perhaps grief? Yes, I have felt grief. There, I've said it. Admitted it."

"But why grief?" Tobias asked. "You've experienced something profound, something extraordinary! I'd be shouting this from the rooftops!"

Tobias didn't understand. How could he? How could any of these people understand?

But I had gone this far and would keep going.

"I was warned many years ago, before the incident, that I must never let my heart rule my head," I continued. "My mentor told me that it would lead to sadness, despair, and perhaps my ruination. I ignored his warnings."

They all fell silent. They looked confused. I ploughed on.

"I've never had, for lack of a better term, a family. That was fine. You can't miss what you've never had. That kept me sane. That kept me content with my lot in life, even when I became the property of the emperor. For me, there would never be a chance of escape, no hope of manumission." I turned my eyes to Tobias. "Someday, Tobias, I truly believe you will be released. It often happens. But not for me. Still, I was content.

"Then I met the Rabbi and his mother, and all the others. They accepted me. Even the one who wished me dead… I knew he would protect me from the hyenas—not because he liked me, but because he loved and respected the Rabbi. If the Rabbi accepted me, my antagonist would do the same.

"I respected the boundaries of the group and stayed on the edge. I knew my presence was scandalous to their hierarchy. Yet they welcomed me. They even trusted me to teach their children. For the first time, I experienced family. My heart ruled my brain. Now that is gone. Just as I was once warned, I'm experiencing what must be grief. It's personal and has nothing to do with accepting who the Rabbi is. I feel loss, but not the loss of him, for the Rabbi is always with me. It's the loss of *them*—living with them, sharing their joy. I will never forget how they cared even for one such as I. That's how I *feel*."

I ran out of words. I was spent.

"Thank you, Darius," spoke the woman who had started this line of question. "That must have been difficult for you, opening up to us. But it's exactly what I needed to hear. I had some reservations about you. Were you using the Rabbi's fame for your own glorification? Now I understand. Now I can accept."

I heard nothing about the apostles, the disciples, or the Rabbi's other followers, including the women and children. I was confined to my desk and the security of the centurion's home in the evenings.

One day, alone in the garden outside the home of my master, I allowed myself to go "away."

To my surprise, Simi bounded into the yard and jumped onto my lap.

Tobias appeared behind the animal. "You have company," he said.

"Hi Darius!" This came from Little Simon. When I got a good look at him, coming around the corner of the building, I realized that he wasn't so little anymore; he had grown. "My dad said I should come and let you know what's been happening."

The centurion followed these guests into the garden.

"Don't worry, sir," Simon assured Marcus. "I was vigilant. I wasn't followed."

"Are you sure you won't consider a career in the military?" My master... was he smiling?

"No, sir. I'm learning to be a fisherman. My grandfather's teaching me." Young Simon sounded proud. "With my dad being away so much, I've got to take care of my mom and sisters."

Tobias brought over a tray with refreshments and a honey cake. Apparently he too was joining us. He poured Simon a glass of juice and cut off a large slab of cake.

"For me, sir?" the young man said. "Thanks! This is so good!"

Simi left my lap to sit at his master's feet.

"There's been some trouble." Simon spoke between bites. "My mom says this is to be expected. Those high priests aren't going to quietly give up their power and wealth! Some angry men killed our friend Stephen because he was talking about the Rabbi. My dad was put in prison by the chief priest, but he's out now. Dad says that the guards forgot to lock the door one day and he simply walked out of jail.

"There have been lots of cures done in the Rabbi's name, of course. Many believe that he is Yahweh's son. Mother Mary, Mary Magdelene, and some of the other ladies are handing out food to the poor, widows, and street kids. Lady Claudia is looking to buy a property, I think in

Jericho, to house widows and orphans. Philip has gone into Samaria to bring the people there the Rabbi's message.

"There is a new member of the high priest's army. My dad says this man is very dangerous! His name is Saul and he's taken over the temple guard. He's been dragging believers out of their houses and throwing them into prison. Dad says we should all start meeting in safer places, not our houses. He says we may have to seek out caves. We have to be careful, for there are many spies these days. If someone seems a bit too eager to get you talking about the Rabbi, you should trace a fish on the ground and see if they react. Believers know this symbol. It means they are part of us. I think that's it…"

Simon trailed off, coming to the end of his report. I think that's it.

"Oh, Olivia really wanted to come too, but it would've been risky," he added. He then turned to Tobias. "Would it be okay if I have another piece? It's so good!"

Growing boys apparently had big appetites. After receiving another piece of cake and a farewell, the young man was gone, loyal black dog at his side.

"He'd make a mighty fine soldier," the centurion muttered as he and Tobias returned to the house, leaving me alone in the garden once again.

I needed solitude. I needed to analyze what I had just learned. Stephen murdered? Followers imprisoned. But of course they had known the risks.

My logical brain deduced that this had been inevitable. Those in power wouldn't yield to this old yet new concept of the Golden Rule. The Rabbi's command was not exclusive. When he said "Do unto others…" it extended beyond the chosen ones, beyond the tribes of Israel. 'Love your enemies,' he had said. 'Share what you have with those less fortunate.' The Rabbi had once joked that it was harder for the rich to enter the kingdom than it would be for a camel to climb through the eye of a needle.

In humour, there was also truth.

Yes, those in power would balk. There would be resistance.

A memory overtook me. Back in Tuscany, Lucien had often been called out to attend to births, whether of humans or animals. He usually got the call when it was too late.

One day, a midwife called for Lucien to assist with a difficult delivery.

Lucien performed his examination. He then looked at me, for I was still quite young, and communicated with only his eyes: this was not good.

He approached the woman's head, gently took her hand, and even more gently explained the situation to her. The woman was exhausted. She was sweating as she laboured to breathe. Her pulse was racing…

Despite myself, I too was assessing the situation.

"Save the child, please," the woman cried out adamantly. "Save the baby. Do whatever you must, but save the child."

"Darius, make the preparations," Lucien said. "I'll go speak with the husband."

Lucien had trained me. I knew what he meant.

I prepared the drink. It was potent. Sometimes the patient would later awaken from the induced sleep. Sometimes not. Most often not.

I wiped the woman's face with a sponge. I had been trained.

"You have yellow hair," she said through the pain, still lucid. "I wonder what colour my child's hair will be?"

"Probably not yellow." I used levity, perhaps inappropriately, but she smiled.

"This physician." She gasped; another pain. "He is proficient?"

"He is, my lady. Very skilled." I brought the cup to her lips, "Lucien explained about this?"

I just wanted to be sure, for this was a potent concoction.

"He did. I will sleep and feel nothing. I understand."

I raised the cup. Little by little, she drank. Then she smiled. I monitored her pulse and her breathing as they each slowed down, as I had been taught.

Soon she was adrift.

When Lucien re-entered the room, his eyes told me which instruments to pass him. We didn't need to speak.

He began the cut.

Once the baby was removed, I passed the towelling and Lucien separated child from mother. The baby wasn't breathing and he began the resuscitation process. He held the neonate by its heels as I cleared the airway. Gently he swayed the babe as if it were a newborn lamb, calf, or piglet. And again I cleared the airway. Lucien began the rubbing…

I checked the mother's pulse. She was dead.

The infant mewed. One life was over; another was beginning.

Lucien handed the child to the midwife, and I handed Lucien the sewing kit.

"You prepare the body," he told me. "I'll speak with the father."

I had been trained and knew how to prepare the body. Smooth the hair. Wash the face. Pull up the blanket, as if the deceased were asleep.

"It's a boy," I whispered in her ear. "He has black hair. He is perfect."

Perhaps she heard.

The father entered, grief on his face, and approached the woman's body. The midwife handed him his son. A look of wonder came over his face.

Lucien and I stood back to watch; our work was done.

As we walked back to the ludus, Lucien spoke. "Darius, in bringing something new into the world, there will be pain, even death, like today. Don't focus on the mother. She willingly gave her life. Focus on the wonderment of the new life."

Lucien had been correct once again. Logically, there would be imprisonments and deaths in the coming years. The old order would resist change. The Rabbi had predicted that his followers would change the world, but there would be birth pains.

I rose from my bench in the centurion's garden. I wasn't watching where I put my feet, and I stubbed my toes. A shock of pain! These were toes that had been broken…

"Damn!"

Just then, I heard the voice of the Rabbi: "I said that the journey wouldn't always be easy."

"Always the clumsy one," replied Lucien. "His head in the clouds. It's a wonder he survived."

The Rabbi laughed. "In the clouds, you say? Yahweh, I Am, me... we dwell above the clouds..."

"Why couldn't it have been just a couple of bee stings," I muttered as I went inside. "Why broken toes?"

The Rabbi was amused.

PART FOUR
Journey

Back in the beginning, the Rabbi had warned me that the journey ahead would not always be easy. Indeed, I sensed that my journey was about to get much more difficult.

I always left the door to my cell open during my workdays, lest the centurion or his optio call on me. On this day, I recognized the two soldiers who came to get me. They were the same ones who had taken me to Claudia in the early days, the first time I'd met her.

I felt the first soldier's fist hit my stomach! I winced. I was not brave.

"Darius, come." It was the voice of my master.

"Yes, sir?"

I didn't look at the men. I kept my head and eyes lowered, silently repeating my mantra.

Breathe, calm, focus.

"I have just received this." Marcus handed me the parchment.

I read the document and realized that the governor was recalling me. These two soldiers were to escort me to Caesarea immediately.

It was most difficult to read the centurion's eyes. He was, after all, a professional soldier and always showed an impassive face. Perhaps it was part of his military training.

"Yes, sir. Understood, sir."

But I didn't understand.

"You will have to wait until tomorrow, as I'll require my scribe's services for the rest of the day," Marcus said to the two soldiers. "My second will see to it that you are both accommodated for the night. Dismissed."

Once they left, my master and I were left alone.

"This comes as a complete surprise to both of us, Darius," he said. "At some point, you were to be recalled to Caesarea, but I never anticipated it would be so soon. Pilate and I trained together. We worked our way up the ranks side by side and are friends. But he is now the governor and my superior."

"Yes, sir, and an order is an order."

The centurion nodded.

"Sir?" I had a request. "It will take some time to clear my desk. There are many reports and much paperwork to complete. May I stay here tonight and work into the night?"

If I were to leave Jerusalem, I would leave all of my work in order. I was obsessive.

"Yes, of course," he said. "I will have Tobias pack up at the residence."

"Thank you, sir."

I returned to my desk.

The morning came too soon. It was time to depart, and the centurion came to my cell. He had brought my bag.

"Darius, you have been an excellent scribe, but also the most annoying, frustrating, and vexing person I have ever encountered," he said. "Yet strangely… I shall miss you. Shalom."

"Thank you, sir."

Breathe, calm, focus.

And so began the trek from Jerusalem to Caesarea. The two soldiers mounted and I followed along, thankfully not limping. I kept my eyes lowered, as these two had little use for me.

I talked to Yahweh in my head, for the Rabbi had said that he was my God too. I admitted that I had willingly agreed to follow the Rabbi, so logically I had no right to complain of the consequences. But I reminded Him of my lack of courage. I acknowledged, however, that I had been gifted with a fine brain and asked for the wisdom to use it effectively.

When the sun was nearing noon, we stopped to rest and water the horses. The commissary had provided food for us to take along, as this was a dirt road with few amenities. One of the soldiers took the mounts to tether and tend. The other stood before me.

I waited for instructions.

"What have you done?" the soldier asked in an unfriendly manner. "Why are we taking you to Caesarea?"

"I do not know, sir. Perhaps you are following orders?"

He was much bigger, taller, and stronger than me, which he proved by lifting me by my tunic. I winced in preparation for the inevitable blow.

The other soldier returned. "Lineus! What are you doing? We were ordered to bring him safely to the governor. If he is bruised or damaged, we'll be the ones on the stinging end of the whip!"

I was dropped roughly to the ground.

"Sit," my antagonist ordered.

I sat.

The man just had to do something, so he kicked me. His boot connected with my foot—the foot with the toes that were still in the final stages of healing. I winced as I felt the colour drain from my face. I tried to control my breathing.

Sorry, Rabbi, but damn, damn, damn—this is going to hurt!

"I just gave him a little nudge with my foot," the one called Lineus declared. "Just a nudge."

"You okay?" the horse-keeping soldier asked. I soon learned his name was Servius.

"No, sir. I think one or two of my toes have been rebroken."

"Lineus!"

"It was just a nudge."

I couldn't eat the rest of that day. I tried to drink, since I had to stay hydrated. I knew I was going to limp—again.

"If he can't walk, you'll be the one walking," Servius told his companion. "He'll be on your horse!"

I could limp. It would be much more slow-going, but I was mobile.

I distracted myself by talking to my friend. *If it had been but a few wasp stings, I would have taken Claudia on the shorter trail. There'd have been no broken toes, and now I wouldn't be hobbling along in pain.*

"*I told you the journey wouldn't always be easy,*" the Rabbi replied, amused. "*You're the one who chose to follow.*"

We wouldn't reach our halfway point, Joppa, by nightfall. Sunset was nearing. There was a cluster of small buildings ahead. The soldiers stopped at the first of these dwellings. We would spend the night here.

A large brown dog barked as we approached the entrance. With raised hackles, the animal charged at us, the intruders. Then it paused… and approached me! I didn't want either soldier to hurt the beast, so I extended my arm and the dog neared, wagging its tail. I bent to scratch its head and ears, as I had done so many times long ago when Lucien and I had been called out to the kennels.

The woman of the house appeared. She had a babe in her arms while a small boy peered out from behind her legs. Another boy, this one a teenager, stood at her side along with a younger girl.

The woman looked frightened to see us.

"We shall be staying here tonight," Servius announced. He pointed to the stone barn. "You and your brood can spend the night there. Boy, take our horses and turn them out in that pen. I assume you have both hay and water?"

When he spoke, this soldier sounded very much like the centurion.

"Lineus, take the scribe to the barn while I check the house." He began to move. "Come, missus. Show me the dwelling."

My guard pushed me into the building. When he found a suitable place, he ordered me to sit and attached one end of a shackle he'd removed from his bag to a ring in the wall; the other shackle enclosed my wrist.

"That should hold you," he remarked.

You really think I could get very far if I tried to escape? I thought. *Illogical!*

The big dog came into the shed and settled down beside me. I scratched his ears and he laid his head on my lap. It was not unpleasant. I had company.

But my foot ached… and that was most unpleasant!

I needed to take my mind off the pain. In search of a diversion, I looked into my shoulder bag, which Tobias had packed. There was a folder… I withdrew it and found a copy of my reports! I decided to read them, curious as I was as to their accuracy.

I was "away," reading, and a child's voice called to me.

"What are you doing?" It was the small boy.

"I am reading, young master."

"Why?"

"For a distraction, young master."

The child settled beside the dog. "Brutus is a watchdog. Brutus doesn't like strangers. How come Brutus likes you?"

"I don't know, young master. Perhaps he senses I would never hurt him?"

The boy noticed the chain holding me in place. "Did you do something bad?"

"I don't think so, young master."

"Did you try to run away?"

"No, young master. That would be a very unwise thing for me to do."

"Then why are the soldiers here?"

"I believe they just needed a place to spend the night."

"But it's our house!"

"I'm sorry, young master." I didn't know what else to say.

The lady of the house and the other children now entered. The mother had a basket and blankets. The older two carried lanterns and jugs.

"It looks like we'll all be sleeping out here tonight," the mother told her children, trying to sound cheerful. "Just like camping."

The older two glared at me, as though I were responsible for this.

"He's not done anything bad," the boy proclaimed in my defence. "He's not tried to run away either. And Brutus likes him."

"And yet our house has been taken over by Romans," said the mother.

"I'm sorry, my lady. My foot is damaged, which is why we had to stop."

Servius now entered. "Do you have something—an ointment or balm—for his foot?" he said to the woman. "It's injured. And he hasn't eaten today or had much liquid. It's important we get him to the governor in Caesarea in good form. I trust you are capable of tending to such matters?"

She nodded. "I shall treat him as one of my own, sir." There was a hint of mockery in her voice.

"Then I shall leave him in your capable hands. Shalom, madam." And with that, the soldier left again

"What have you done?" The mother looked fearful.

"I only obeyed orders, my lady, I really don't understand myself. I am sorry."

"John, go to Anna and explain. She'll know what to do." The mother sent the teenager off—to a neighbour, I assumed. "Is your foot badly damaged?"

"I fear it may be, my lady. It's an old injury. Broken toes… there's not much one can do. They take time to heal."

A man—perhaps the woman's husband?—now entered the barn.

"What's going on?" he demanded. "John says soldiers have taken over the house. And who is this slave?" He sounded both angry and worried at the same time.

"The soldiers are staying the night," his wife explained. "They're taking him to Caesarea, but he's injured and had to stop for the night. We will be fine out here. I have food, blankets, and lanterns. It'll be like camping." The mother was again trying to make this sound like an adventure. "It's only for the night. They'll be gone in the morning."

The boy next to the dog spoke up. "Brutus likes him. He's not done anything bad and he's not a runaway. And he can read."

Apparently I had one supporter amongst those present.

The husband towered above me. I should have stood—he was free-born—but I couldn't, so I simply lowered my head and eyes, as was proper.

Breathe, calm, focus.

"You're a slave?"

"Yes, sir."

"A Gentile?"

"Yes, sir."

"A runaway?"

"No, sir."

"Why then have two soldiers taken over my house?"

"I injured my foot, delaying the trip, sir."

He looked down and saw the papers spread out in front of me. "What are you reading? *Why* are you reading? You're a slave."

"I am, sir, but I'm also a scribe. I was reading a copy of my reports. I needed a diversion and am checking whether my words have been accurately copied."

The man returned to sit with his family.

"Perhaps we should eat," suggested the mother. "But first, let's go wash."

I knew this was a Jewish more, to cleanse before eating.

As the family went to wash, the dog stayed by my side. Meanwhile, my foot ached! I closed my eyes and I drifted off. Pain can make a person sleep… a mercy.

I awoke with a start to see the family eating. It was early evening.

"Feeling any better?" The mother's voice was not unfriendly.

"Perhaps, my lady. Thank you."

She approached and knelt in front of me with some food. The girl too had a cup.

"You must eat," the mother instructed.

Brutus was now alert.

"No, Brutus, that's not for you. Come, I'll feed you." The girl ordered the dog away and he followed her.

It was a typical Jewish meal—dried meat, bread and oil, and dried fruit. I took a sip from the cup and realized it was a mixture of wine, juice, and water. The pain had taken away my appetite.

"It's me, my lady," I said by way of explanation. "Not your cooking."

"Try harder. You want me to get into trouble with these Romans?"

"No, my lady."

We were interrupted by Lineus, who unfastened the wrist shackle and ordered me to follow him.

I limped out of the barn into the night air, finding it cool and fresh. I was happy that it seemed I'd have the opportunity to perform evening ablutions. For that, I was grateful—for my escort, not so much.

"Lady Claudia won't be there to protect you in Caesarea." His voice was hard.

It seemed he had little use for me, and I feared him. I was not brave.

When we returned to the shed, after I'd had a chance to clean myself, there were many more people than before.

"Who are you?" Lineus demanded of the new arrivals in his most soldier-like voice. "Why are you here?"

A rather large woman confronted him. I admired her courage. Roman soldier or not, she faced him defiantly.

"The other soldier charged our Rachel with making sure your prisoner ate. Then she was to treat his injury," she shot back. "We're all kin. Ask for one and you get all of us. I have broth. Sarah has made a honey cake. Rachel's problem is our problem, sir!" She was in his face; she was formidable.

"And the children?" Although taken aback, Lineus still attempted to assert his authority.

"You expect us to leave our babes unattended?" The stout woman wasn't backing down. "What kind of a mother did you have, sir?"

Lineus was struggling to maintain control. "And what of these men?"

"You expect us, with our little ones, to go out into the night unescorted? Really, sir!"

"See to it that you don't stay long." Lineus reshackled my wrist, then reached to pick up the cake and a jar of wine. "I'll take this and this."

He left the barn.

The formidable woman approached me. "Let's see that foot," she said in a demanding, but not intimidating, tone of voice.

I explained why I had left the sandal on, but she ignored my words and removed the shoe. The foot was indeed swollen and bruised.

"John, the salve," she said.

The teen handed the formidable woman a jar.

"Are you not concerned about defilement, my lady?" I asked. "I'm a Gentile."

"Do I worry about defilement when I rub an unction on an ox or a donkey? In my experience, the patient is the last one to be allowed to treat himself. He's far too gentle when a firm hand is required."

I tried not to wince as she applied the treatment.

"There, that should help. Now drink this."

She had given an order and I had to obey.

I took a sip… and stopped.

"You think I'm trying to poison you?" she asked, adamant.

"No, my lady. That would be illogical. But I detect the flavour of an herb I'm not familiar with."

"You have a good palate. Yes, there is a medicinal herb in the broth. It will help you sleep. That injury is painful. You will need to sleep…"

She trailed off, and I realized she had stopped speaking on account of the expression on my face.

"That's it! Someone has tried to kill you," she said with a burst of insight. "I saw a flash of fear in your eyes. Don't deny it. This explains a great deal. But why would anyone want to kill you?"

I tried levity. "Perhaps an aversion to the colour of my hair, my lady?"

The father now spoke. "I suspect those papers have something to do with his present situation—and since we're the ones being inconvenienced, we have the right to know just what this is all about. If you're not a criminal or a runaway, you owe us an explanation."

I had to reply, but how much information should I divulge?

Yahweh, wisdom please, I silently prayed.

"I was ordered to follow and record what the one called the Rabbi taught, where he travelled, and what he did," I began. "Rome is always concerned about crowd size and possible insurrections. I am fluent in many languages, including Aramaic. Jesus allowed me to follow him to witness where he went and what he did, and to file my reports. I always respected the social and religious boundaries. I was accepted into the group. In the end, the Rabbi was put to death. Pontius Pilate gave the order to execute him, but the high priest was the instigator. Now that the Rabbi has been crucified, I assume that my services are no longer required. That's why I am being recalled to Caesarea."

"But why two soldiers? Surely you could find your way to Caesarea unescorted." The father didn't seem satisfied with my explanation. "And why an assassination attempt?"

"I can only assume that the governor suspects the high priest of looking upon me as some kind of threat. Perhaps because I'm fluent in many languages, the governor feels I am somehow valuable? If you lift the sleeve of my tunic, you will see the imperial mark. So perhaps I am to be returned to Rome. I really don't know, sir. It's not my place to ask."

One of the men suggested that I read some of my reports, which I did, selecting a few of the Rabbi's teachings, including the accounts of healings. I also shared stories of Jesus raising the teenage boy and Lazarus from the dead.

The formidable woman inquired as to whether these two people were actually dead.

"They were, my lady. I'm a good scribe, but I'm also medically trained. I've been performing the death checks since I was a stripling. My mentor insisted on this so I would become accustomed to death. These two were dead. Now they live."

Another asked whether the rumours about the Rabbi were actually true: had he risen?

This was going to be difficult. Surely they would think me mad if I told the truth. But my logical brain insisted that I speak. I had seen what I'd seen and had to truthfully respond.

I took a breath. "Yes, sir, you may disbelieve, but on two occasions I met the Rabbi-risen." My logical brain warned me not to mention anything involving Claudia. "Many have seen, talked with, and eaten with the risen Jesus. He conquered death, returned to reassure his followers, and has since returned to his Father, Yahweh and the I Am."

"You believe then that this Jesus of Nazareth is the Messiah?" a man asked.

"Sir, I'm not a qualified priest or rabbi. I know little of gods other than that the Romans and Greeks have their household gods, as well as the Egyptians and many other cultures too. I learned about Jewish mores from my time in Israel. I am, however, fortunate to have been well-educated and a person of science. As such, I formulated a hypothesis. Is Jesus of Nazareth the son of Yahweh come to earth? I tested this based on the data I witnessed and formulated a conclusion: the Rabbi indeed is the son of Yahweh come to earth to fulfill a mission—to teach, to die, to redeem, and to rise from the grave. He has now been reunited with Yahweh and the I Am. This is, of course, my conclusion. I'm sorry that I've caused you inconvenience, that your lives have been disrupted."

"You have a name?" the formidable woman asked.

"Yes, my lady. Darius."

"Well, Darius, not much happens around here," she said. "Yes, this has been an unexpected event, but it's actually quite interesting and informative. I for one wish you well." She began to gather the young people. "Come, children, it's past your bedtimes. Shalom, everyone. Shalom."

After their goodbye hugs, we were soon left with the original family and the big brown dog. They distributed blankets and even gave one to me. The dog rested his head on my lap and I heard the mother sing a soft lullaby. I'd never heard anything like it before. Was this what a mother did, sing softly to her children at night? It wasn't an unpleasant way to end the day.

I awoke with a start! The toddler was on my lap. He seemed quite fascinated with my hair; I suspect the colour was unfamiliar to him. Then he pounced on the sleeping dog, who now also woke with a start.

I had to smile. It wasn't an unpleasant way to begin a day.

The mother was also awake, and she too smiled. The big dog was now serving as the toddler's pony. She rose, cradled the babe for a few moments, and left to begin her morning chores. She had flour to grind, bread to bake, porridge to cook, and a young one to wash and change.

All were astir, including the Romans. After a flurry of morning activity, it was time to resume our journey.

The father approached me. "Darius, take this. It will help." He gave me a shepherd's staff.

"Thank you, sir." I was grateful.

"I apologize for our intrusion," Servius told the man. "I trust we have caused no damage."

We continued on. Upon reaching Joppa, we picked up a proper Roman iter, a paved road. Even at a slower pace, we should reach Caesarea by nightfall. Soon I would find out the reason for my sudden recall, as well as where my journey would take me next.

Breathe, calm, focus.

It was quite late when we reached the fortress. It was huge, housing thousands of military and staff. The sentry allowed us entry, and the soldiers found a cell for me once the horses were turned over to the hostler.

My foot ached! The walk had been long and I was exhausted. But before I fell asleep that night, I asked the Rabbi once again, *Why broken toes, sir?*

I awoke the next morning and set to the task of looking presentable before my appearance later that day before the governor. I was allowed to bathe, and I even received a fresh tunic. For this, I was grateful. I was obsessive. It felt so good to finally have a proper bath and rinse the desert sand from my hair!

The soldiers who had brought me to the fortress were now standing near the bath's entrance, planning a reunion with some of their comrades once I was returned to the cell to which I'd been assigned. I quickly and discreetly towel-dried, hoping no one would pay attention to me.

But Servius saw me and saw the scarring on my body.

"Someone laced into you," the guard said, pulling the sheet lower to expose the marks. "Not a very professional job."

I heard Lucien in my head: *"Of course he'd be interested. Soldiers are trained in the use of disciplinary aids."*

Breathe, calm, focus.

"I told you this one had a dark past!" Lineus sounded triumphant. "What did you do to deserve the whipping?"

I remained silent. My eyes were lowered, as was proper, but I saw his boot edge closer to my foot—the one with the obvious damage.

I winced involuntarily.

"I asked you a question!" Lineus threatened. He really had no use for me.

"I spoke out of turn, sir. It was long ago and far away."

Servius sounded more interested in me. "I'm not sure there's a dark side to this one... more a deep side. The scribe knows something."

I said nothing.

It was a relief to don the tunic, fine linen as it was, even though it marked me as property of the emperor, a mere asset. The tunic hid the marks, reminders of my failure as a friend, as a person. The embroidery marked me as a scribe.

Thank You, Yahweh, that they didn't pursue the matter, I prayed. *The past is the past.*

I wondered about the future, and even feared where it might take me. I was not brave.

"Have you put that salve on your foot?" Lineus demanded. Why was he suddenly concerned about my well-being?

"Yes, sir," I replied, but I still limped. Such injuries required time to heal.

My escorts were praetorian guards familiar with the fortress; they led me through the hallways to the chamber where Pontius Pilate was seated. They were well familiar with the palace and soon traversed its maze of hallways and atria.

Suddenly another guard opened a massive ornate door, allowing the three of us to enter a grand chamber.

As we entered, I immediately saw Pilate, as well as a much older soldier present with him.

"Lineus, Servius... you know Rufus?" the governor inquired. He then turned his attention to me, unable to help noticing the way I walked over the unforgiving marble floor. "Darius, you are limping."

"It's nothing, sir. An old injury." I saw no point in implicating anyone.

"I would have you consult with the base physician, but apparently you are one. Marcus has kept me apprised. Why was this not noted earlier?"

"No one ever asked, sir."

Pilate chuckled. "I understand why Marcus found you so annoying. However, your work as a scribe has been excellent—your reports timely, informative, well-written, and offering no interpretation. Just the facts. But it's not your work, Darius, that brings you here today. It's you. There has already been one attempt on your life and I cannot risk having you in Israel. Lady Claudia is already planning to make you her secretary. I cannot allow that. Your proximity would put her in danger. No, I simply cannot allow that!

"While my wife is currently away, I've arranged to send you to a post in northern Gaul. I know the commander. He'll be glad to have your services as a physician. You will be under constant guard until the ship is set to sail. Lineus, Servius, and Rufus will take shifts protecting you."

The governor turned to the trio of guards.

"Everything he eats or drinks, make sure it's safe," the governor ordered. "Spies are everywhere. Eat off-base if necessary. If any harm comes to him, it'll be your heads on pikes. The three of you will also escort Darius aboard ship and see him to Vetera. Rufus, you will retire there. Your twenty years of service will be up and your pension awaits. And once Darius is handed over, Lineus and Servius, you will return here. Any questions?"

Lineus spoke up first. "Sir, why us?"

"Lady Claudia will be angry enough when she finds out what I've done. It will appease her to know that her most trusted guards are with Darius. My wife highly values the scribe." Pilate again turned to observe me. "Darius, the base physician is packing a trunk of supplies. There will be no surgery where you're going. He wants to meet with you to go over details."

"Understood, sir."

And I did. Claudia had to be protected; my life was inconsequential.

"When does this ship depart?" Rufus asked.

"In three days, the tide will be right."

"I suggest we go into town and celebrate" the one called Rufus called to the other two guards as we headed out of the palace. I was limping along, sandwiched between Servius and Lineus. "We just landed a plum of an assignment!"

"We're going to the ends of the empire" complained Lineus. "The tribes in Britannia are wild beasts."

But Rufus was feeling jubilant. "We're not going there! There's a river between. Besides, since Julius Caesar went to his ancestors there's been no trouble with the Blue Warriors. Heck, they're trading allies with the empire."

"I get seasick," Servius said unhappily.

We soon found ourselves at a local tavern.

They had me sit with my back to the wall for security. They ordered sour wine, cheese, bread, and other items that weren't easily poisoned.

"He doesn't drink wine," Servius observed as the server placed the cups.

"Good. More for us," replied Rufus. He was in the mood to talk. "Pilate said there's been one attempt on your life. Why would anyone want to kill a scribe?"

"I don't know, sir. I had no opportunity to inquire."

"You've got slave-speak down to an artform!" the older soldier roared in amusement.

"It must have something to do with Lady Claudia," Servius said. "Pilate doesn't want you near her."

I said nothing.

Servius narrowed his eyes. "That day when Lady Claudia talked to you alone, she wasn't chastising you. She wanted information—about that Rabbi character!"

I said nothing.

Thankfully, Rufus seemed ready for a nap. "Drink up. We'd best be returning."

It was quite late in the evening when Lineus entered my cell. The fortress, particularly the barracks, was all quiet.

"Come," Lineus said. "The governor wants you."

Lineus led me to a very different room, one that was smaller. Perhaps it was part of his bedchamber.

We soon stood before Pilate in his chamber. Lineus stood by my side.

"You may leave," Pilate ordered the soldier.

Lineus hesitated. "Sir, is it safe—"

"What's the scribe going to do? Bore me to death with an explanation of Pythagorean principles? Out!"

I actually found these theories exciting, but of course I was somewhat odd. I remained silent. We were alone and I was unsettled.

Breathe, calm, focus.

"Come, sit." Pilate indicated the flask on the table. "Want some?"

"No, sir, thank you. I am content."

But I sat. An order had been given, and I almost always obeyed.

"But I am not content!" the governor said. "I need to talk to someone. Lady Claudia and Marcus… they both said they talked with, even ate with, the Rabbi—and yet I ordered his crucifixion! I didn't have your courage…"

"Courage, sir? I am hardly brave." I had no idea where this conversation was leading.

Breathe, calm, focus.

"You had the courage to change the wording on his sign."

"Yes, sir, I did."

"When that annoying high priest Caiphas came complaining and demanding that the sign be rewritten, I had the 'courage' to take the credit for the few words you omitted. I didn't have the courage to save an innocent man's life. Now Marcus and my wife say he has risen! History will forever look upon me as the one who killed the Son of God!"

Pilate looked beaten, and I felt that I should speak, even though he was so far above my station.

"Sir, Marcus was the exactor mortis," I said. "He conducted the execution. Yet the Rabbi asked to meet with him, to show that he bears no grudge and seeks no vengeance. The Rabbi met with Lady Claudia, perhaps in your stead, for it would have been impossible for you to go to the rendezvous. I was at the execution myself. His last words weren't angry. The Rabbi called to his Father, saying, 'Forgive them. They don't know what they're doing.' Perhaps instead of blaming you, some wise ones in the future will realize that you were an instrument, part of his redemptive act?"

"Still, I needed to talk to someone. It's been like a millstone around my neck." Pilate didn't look consoled. "I will be forever hated. I should have handled this differently."

In my head, I prayed for the Rabbi to console him. I didn't have the words. I understood Pilate's guilt; I shared his guilt.

The next morning brought another welcome bath. The heat of the water soothed the foot. It was indeed swollen and bruised.

Servius decided that we'd breakfast in the barracks hall. The food was served in dishes set out on a communal table. Again, this provided less chance of poisoning.

A soldier's first meal of the day was never appealing! I understood their need to replenish their salt intake, but porridge with herbs and fermented fish sauce made from intestines? Sour wine for breakfast? At least there were breads and dried fruit.

"You're a picky eater," Servius observed.

"Yes, sir." Another item to be added to the very long list of things others found annoying about me.

I was to spend the day with the fortress physician and familiarize myself with the equipment and supplies necessary to establish an infirmary at my new posting.

The infirmary was within the fortress and my guard had no trouble finding it despite the vastness of the place.

The physician rose to greet Servius and myself as we entered his office.

"You must be Darius," the man said. "The scribe who is actually a physician."

"Yes, sir."

"Where did you train?"

"Alexandria, sir."

"Surreptitiously, I assume."

"Yes, sir."

"Your master wanted to be a physician?"

"No, sir. His focus was to have been business and math."

"Yet you obtained a medical degree?"

"Yes, sir. I earned it in memory of my mentor. I also studied business and math for my master."

"Quite the accomplishment. I'm impressed. Yet you were assigned a scribe?"

"Yes, sir."

"Not a physician?"

"No, sir."

"Why?"

"No one asked about my medical training, sir."

"You're very odd!"

"So I've been told, sir."

"Please, call me Eutropius."

"I cannot do that, sir."

"Why not?"

"It wouldn't be proper, sir."

Eutropius shook his head. "Shall we get on with it?"

"Yes, sir."

As the morning wore on, it was pleasant to handle familiar instruments and pack familiar unctions, medicinals, bandages, drugs, and herbs. It was comforting to itemize, list, and record everything that was packed into the shipping crates.

When we stopped for cena, the main meal, Servius suggested that we eat off-base for safety.

During the meal, Servius and Eutropius conversed. I preferred it that way.

"Darius?"

My head shot up, for Eutropius was now speaking to me.

"I am curious," the physician said. "I've read your reports. You witnessed some amazing things. As a physician, are you absolutely certain there was no trickery, sleight of hand, or mass hysteria?"

"I am very certain there was no deceit, sir."

"As to those risings from the dead, are you certain the corpses were indeed corpses?"

"Yes, sir. I've been performing death checks and preparing bodies since I was a youngster. The bodies... they were dead."

I replayed memories of Lucien going out to inform and support the family members of the deceased while I checked once more to be certain of the death and prepare the body before Lucien returned with the bereaved. I had seen far too many bodies.

"That must have been an amazing experience," Eutropius said.

"It was, sir."

As we walked back to the fortress, Eutropius couldn't help but notice that I was limping.

"It's nothing, sir. Just a couple of broken toes."

"Would you like something for the pain?" he asked.

"No, sir."

"Why?"

"It was ingrained in me, sir: no wine, no alcohol, no drugs or sedations. A physician must always be clear-headed. I have kept my promise to my mentor. I owe him that."

"You must be the only person I know who has ever kept a promise."

I thought of Lucien. It was the least I could do to honour that promise.

The cart was waiting, packed with supplies. Eutropius had added a few bags of lime and instructed me to spread the powder in the boat, below the spot where the rowers were chained. He explained that the powder reduced the chance of disease.

I cringed. That's exactly why I preferred being a scribe!

The drover suggested that I sit beside him as he enjoyed the company. My three guards then mounted and we set off for the pier and the large sailing ship that would take us north to Gesacorium.

When the goods were loaded—as well as a few passengers, mostly men engaged in trade—it was farewell to Israel.

You never mentioned that my journey would involve sailing the Mare Internum, Rabbi, I thought.

"You never asked." The Rabbi sounded amused.

The governor had arranged that we be accommodated in the finest room that the cargo vessel provided. Rufus was delighted, proclaiming again what a dream assignment this was for a career soldier like him.

And then the ship set sail.

Servius had worried about seasickness, but in the first week of the voyage it struck not him but Lineus and Rufus. As for myself, I kept busy dosing them with calming herbs, holding compresses on their foreheads as they retched, and emptying pails of vomit.

Ugh. I preferred life as a scribe.

One evening, Servius and I sat on the deck. We both needed the fresh air while the other two slept. I had given them medicinals.

"What's it like being you?" the soldier asked.

"Me, sir?"

"Yes."

"I don't understand the question, sir, or how to respond. I have no point of reference. I have always been *me.*"

"You think oddly."

"Yes, sir."

"Lineus has hurt you, yet you tend to him with kindness. A normal person would let him sleep in his own bile, yet you take no revenge."

"That would be illogical, sir. A physician's oath is to do no harm. To leave Lineus in such a state would contradict that oath. Illogical."

In my head I added, *And the Rabbi taught that we must extend kindness to those who hurt us.*

"You are unusual," Servius mused again. "The one you were sent to follow and record, the Nazarene… what was he like?"

"Do you mean what *did* he like, sir?" I couldn't quite understand the nature of the soldier's query.

"What kind of person was he? If he did all you recorded him as doing, including those healings… if he was so popular, was he, I don't know, 'un-human' somehow?"

"No, sir, the Rabbi was very human. He laughed, ate, slept, and felt pain if he stubbed his toe. He was patient, full of empathy, and couldn't tolerate hypocrisy. When the demands became overwhelming, he'd take a few from his inner circle, or go off by himself to a solitary spot to rest and recharge. He was normal in all respects."

"Yet you witnessed many abnormal events."

"Indeed, but always in his Father's name, sir. He was very humble and acknowledged openly that these happenings occurred through Yahweh."

"And yet he was crucified."

"His mission, sir, was a redemptive act. It was his journey. He accepted that assignment."

"He must have a dim view of soldiers."

"No, sir, not at all. He once said that soldiers should act fairly. He bore no ill will toward anyone—except for hypocrites."

Servius adopted a more serious tone. "Darius, are the rumours true? Did he who was dead by crucifixion, did he… rise from the tomb?"

Instinctively I wrapped my arms more firmly around my knees, as though hiding.

Why do they keep asking me that?

I remained silent, staring at the ship's plankboards.

"Please, Darius, I'm not ordering you," the soldier asked with sincerity. "I'm asking you as an equal."

"Sir, we are hardly equals."

"Maybe not by birth, but what you know, what you have witnessed… I feel this somehow elevates you. Even for a few minutes, could you not speak openly to me?"

I took a deep breath. Servius had been kind to me, and he had intervened on my behalf. Perhaps I did owe him something.

Breathe, calm, focus.

"He lives," I said without looking up. "The Rabbi… he lives."

"You have seen him, the one we crucified?" Servius didn't mock, but there was an edge of scepticism in his tone.

I kept my arms firmly around my knees. "Yes, sir, I have."

"Perhaps it was a dream, a ghost in your imagination?"

"That's what I thought when I first encountered the Rabbi-risen. Perhaps I had fallen, was concussed, or in a dream-like state. Perhaps this was a chimera, an aura, a phantom?"

Servius of course asked the inevitable: "How did I know the encounter was real?"

"Please, sir, I do feel that I owe you something for intervening on my behalf. But I beg you, sir, to keep this between us. I have told no one, shown no one, my mark of shame." I looked up at him as an equal.

Servius looked confused. "Of course, Darius, on my honour as a soldier of the emperor. Your secret shall remain just that."

I trusted him. "I doubted. The Rabbi teased me. And then he proved that what was happening was indeed real. I still wear the mark of that proof."

I raised the sleeve of my tunic. There, just above the mark of the emperor of the earthly realm, rested the mark of the Rabbi's two fingers, thumb and index, where he had pinched me to prove that he was the Rabbi-risen.

"The marks have never changed, never faded," I said. "It's a reminder of my scepticism, my mark of shame."

Servius said nothing as he looked at my arm. "Darius, I was correct. What you have seen, what you know… you are truly elevated."

I could feel my face redden. "No, sir, I am not."

I had tried to explain to the captain of the vessel that I had been instructed to powder the lower area of the ship with lime to stem the spread of disease. The man was adamant that no one, not Tiberius himself, could gain access to any part of his ship without permission—and as a slave and under guard, I would definitely be denied access to any area of the boat not designated for passengers!

His refusal caused me grief. Under what horrendous conditions were the galley slaves kept? Were they fed adequately? Were they not rested? Were they tended to when hurt or ill? The only thing I could do was ask Yahweh to watch over them, and thank Yahweh that I was not among them.

I resolved to leave the lime with instructions on how to use it. Perhaps the captain resented a mere slave approaching him and would use the powder once I was no longer aboard his vessel.

Lineus and Rufus soon found their sea legs and we were able to join the few other passengers for meals and company. These were tradesmen, and our presence among them—well, my presence—had been unexpected. Three soldiers to guard one slave? Rufus, the gregarious one, was soon in their midst asking questions about where we were heading, telling tales of his life as a cavalryman. I admired his ease amongst strangers.

It was an uneventful sailing and the ship eventually docked at the naval base at Gesoriacum.

I could hear the Rabbi: *"You chose to follow me. Actions have consequences. Welcome to Gaul."*

Lineus and Servius went ashore to obtain horses from the relay station. Rufus decided we should explore the area while awaiting their return and the unloading of the crates.

Gesoriacum was like every port—busy, with traders bartering and vendors hawking their wares. I listened to the sounds and dialects, a musical mixture of Greek, Latin, and the local language. I enjoyed the variety. This place would be interesting. I also noted a mixture of clothing styles, whether they were Roman tunics or local garb. In particular, there was a very unusual sight: men wearing trousers of a colour and striping I'd never seen, under very short tunics. Odd but interesting.

A cart had been arranged to transport not only the infirmary crates but also other supplies ordered destined for the post to which we were to travel far to the north and inland from the sea.

At first I joined the drover, but before long we were also joined by Rufus. I was thankful. He liked to talk.

The road led past the port, many oddly shaped dwellings, and more familiar villa-styled manors with extensive vineyards and orchards. The signs of habitation thinned as we headed north, though. We encountered only a few small villages and holdings, lots of forest, and slightly undulating terrain.

It took several days to reach our destination. The landscape, so unlike Tuscany or the places I'd seen in Israel, was heavily treed and sparsely populated. The wildness of this place left me feeling unsettled.

The fort at Vetera itself was walled, not of stone but timber. The sentry allowed us to pass.

Our arrival was expected and we were escorted to the legate, the senior officer. He dealt first with the soldiers. Rufus was given instructions as to how to pension out; the other two were told where to accommodate and rest before their return to Caesarea. They were all dismissed.

Now for my instructions. I stood, as was proper, with my head and eyes lowered.

Breathe, calm, focus.

"So you're the scribe-physician?" asked the legate.

"Yes, sir."

"Darius?"

"Yes, sir."

"Marcus and Pilate speak highly of your skills, yet here you are at the far ends of the empire."

"Yes, sir."

"Very odd."

I said nothing.

My instructions were simple: set up an infirmary, treat soldiers, and tend to villagers and the locals. Basically, I was on my own, with no centurion to answer to and a legate who seemed unconcerned about my presence.

When I was dismissed, a soldier showed me to the area designated as the infirmary. The crates from the ship had been deposited inside.

"Thank you, sir," I politely said to my escort.

"I'm not a sir, sir. I'm Natilis. I've been assigned to help you unpack and set up the infirmary."

"I am but a mere slave. Please, sir, it is not proper for you to refer to me as *sir*."

"I disagree, sir. You are educated?"

"Yes, sir."

"You are a qualified physician?"

"Yes, sir."

"That, sir, places you above me, as I can neither read nor write. I am just a farm boy who has older brothers and no other prospect but to join the army."

"The fact remains, sir, that you are freeborn. Ergo, you are of a higher station. Please, sir, refer to me as Darius, physician. Or call me Sponge, Sparrow, or Oyster… any form of address but *sir*."

"Yes, sir."

I was totally perplexed!

Natilis flashed a big grin. Levity?

We began unpacking the crates, but my helper was of little help since he was illiterate. The vials of salves and herbs all had to be itemized, checked off, and placed correctly on the dispensary's shelves. They were labelled and accounted for; I was obsessive.

My aide was at least useful in arranging cots and bedrolls, filling amphoras with water, and bringing in firewood. The time passed quickly—and silently.

"Sir," Natilis prompted.

I startled and took a deep breath. "Yes, sir?" I replied politely.

"I've made us tea. It's time for a break. Come."

He'd issued an order, so I followed him outside. We sat on the step. The fort was quiet.

Natilis smiled broadly. "Where did you come from, sir?"

"I don't understand, sir. Questions like these are confusing—"

"Where was your last posting?"

"Jerusalem, sir."

"You were a physician for King Herod?"

"No, sir. A scribe. My master there was a centurion."

"Why a mere scribe?"

"I do not question, sir. I obey orders." Hopefully that answer would suffice.

"You must have done something *really* above your station to be sent to the far borders of Gaul!" Natilis insisted.

"No, sir, I simply obey orders. Perhaps we should continue with the unpacking, sir?"

"There's a story inside you, sir, and nothing interesting happens here. I will eventually find out…"

I had Natilis unpack and stack the various dressings, sponges, and towelling. No special skills were required for that. In the meantime, I unpacked my few personal items in the small cell designated as my sleeping quarters.

From time to time, I took out the copy of my reports and read them. I often referred to the Rabbi's words; these kept me grounded. These reports and all they revealed about Israel, the Rabbi, Mother Mary, the disciples, and the children… well, it was all true. These events had really happened. I could place myself within these memories, and it felt somewhat like being "away."

"Sir?" Natilis again—and again, I winced. "It's time to eat. Come, join us. On the way, I can show you the quartermaster's office. You will need warmer clothing. The rainy season nears."

My presence caused a bit of a stir. Everyone had been aware that the post was to receive a physician, but I was perhaps not quite the one they were expecting.

"This is our physician?"

"He hardly looks the part."

"He's a slave!"

"Slaves can be physicians."

"What did he do to be sent here?"

Yes, my appearance resulted in a great deal of perplexion among the soldiers. I tried to shut out these reactions as we arrived in the dining hall.

"Darius! We were going to come and say farewell, but here you are," Rufus called to me from the table he shared with Lineus and Servius. "Join us."

Natilis and a few of his mates who had fallen into our wake appeared to have no objection. We took our seats at the table.

"You know our physician?" one soldier asked the visiting guards.

"Oh, Servius and I have a long association with Darius," replied Lineus. "A long and colourful relationship." He gave me a nudge with his elbow.

Natilis inquired why three soldiers from so far away would be required to transport just one slave all the way to northern Gaul.

Rufus loved to talk! And he talked. Soon everyone knew that my life was in danger and I hadn't been able to remain anywhere near Pilate's wife.

Yahweh, please, I prayed for wisdom. *Should I remain silent? What should I do?*

Rabbi replied: *"Breathe, calm, focus."*

Late that evening, I heard a knock on my cell door. It was Natilis.

"You all settled, sir?" he asked.

"Yes, thank you, sir."

The soldier glanced around the space. "I sleep in a barracks, but this is much nicer. Are you reading?"

"I am, sir."

His gaze fell on the clay sparrow figurine that Olivia had gifted to me.

"Oh, you have a sparrow," he remarked. "Is this your family god?"

"No, sir. A gift."

In my head I added, *There is only one God, Yahweh, the great I Am—and the Rabbi.*

"You have a lot of parchments!" Natilis's eyes widened at all my documents.

"Yes, I do, sir."

"You don't talk much."

"No, sir."

"The men asked me to say, 'Welcome to Vetera.' And, sir, anyone of any importance who is sent here has a history. A past. We mean no harm. The men... we're just curious."

Finally, Natalis left me in peace.

Thank you, Rabbi, I prayed.

The young soldier's words could be disruptive. The past was the past; in that, Natilis was correct. It was wise to look ahead, not backward. Lucien had often said the same after a difficult day. This was my new journey.

"Oh, and sir..."

I looked up in dismay to see that Natilis had returned!

Breathe, calm, focus, I reminded myself. *He is freeborn. I must show respect.*

"Yes, sir," I said, again trying to sound polite.

"The men were asking... if it's not too much, in your free time, would you consider scribing letters home for some of us?" Natilis gave me another of his grins. "You are, we hear, also a scribe."

"Yes, sir." Perhaps now I could get back to my reading.

"Oh, and one last thing. The kitchen staff suspect you may be the one who wrote the adventures of the one called Jesus. The officers would read the reports, but the kitchen staff couldn't help but overhear. If so, would you perhaps share these words with the men... sir?"

You do realize, as a freeborn, that you legally have the right to order me to do so?

But I said nothing, and soon Natilis left again.

I resumed reading.

Thank You, Yahweh, I prayed. *I am not a priest, nor a rabbi, nor a disciple, nor an apostle. I am not trained.*

The Rabbi was not amused. *"Really?"*

The infirmary was soon operative and soldiers came for treatment. These were mostly horse-soldiers patrolling the border, maintaining a Roman presence in the area, a reminder to the locals that Gaul was controlled by the Eagle. Their injuries often consisted of simple boils and sores from too many hours astride their mounts, easy to treat but unpleasant for both patient and myself.

As for carpenters and kitchen staff, their occupational hazards required dressings, stitching, and unctions. A few locals also came, perhaps more out of curiosity; word had spread about the yellow-haired slave-physician.

When the rainy season arrived, the air turned cold and raw. I had grown accustomed to desert rain, so this was bone-chilling.

With the change in season came the inevitable illnesses of cough, congestion, and fever. More cots were required. More salve for chests. More herbs for teas. More heat for boiling linens. I spent days and nights among the sick—exactly why medicine had never been my first choice of career.

I had little time, however, to muse. Lucien was always in my head: *"You have patients. Move!"*

When spring arrived, the illness abated. I had not lost a patient. For this, I thanked Yahweh.

There came a day when I was called to a difficult birthing. The village midwife required assistance. Physicians were called only under dire circumstances.

I dreaded my duty this day, but I responded.

The child was born too small, too blue, and too still. I rubbed, swayed, and cleared airways, but it was futile. I wrapped the tiny bundle in a blanket and tried to make the inert babe appear as one asleep. I then handed the stillborn child to the distraught mother. Her anguish stabbed my heart.

"I am so sorry, my lady," I said in consolation. "If only I were more skilled. I am so sorry."

I couldn't return directly to the fort, since I needed time to process and deal with my sense of guilt. Had I missed something? I needed time to grieve.

I soon found myself in a quiet glade where I sat and prayed. I went "away."

"You are troubled, young man?" The stranger's voice called me back to the present.

I looked up to see a figure in a long robe. He also had a long beard.

"Yes, sir," I said, rising. "I'm sorry if I have intruded. It's been a… a difficult day. I needed a few minutes to regroup. I'm sorry for trespassing. I shall return to my base."

"No, please. Sit." The old gentleman spoke in a kind voice. "Tell me what is distressing you so."

"I lost a patient today. A stillborn, I couldn't revive the child. The babe… dead."

"You are a physician?"

"Yes, sir, I am."

"Surgeons can only do so much. Then it's up to the gods."

"Yes, sir, but perhaps if I were more skilled…?"

"I am Cyfner. You are?"

"Darius, sir."

"You must come from farther north, judging by your colour."

"No, sir. I was birthed near Rome."

I explained my start in life—the notched ear indicating that I was slaveborn, as well as the imperial mark, establishing me as property of the Eagle. I had no connection to lands beyond Italia, but I had been east to Alexandria and spent years in Israel.

The old gentleman had no knowledge of the exact location of these places, so I scratched a rough map out on the dirt. He was interested. I explained about the stone houses of the Israelites and magnificent structures of Egypt, Jerusalem, and Rome.

Time passed quickly and eventually I had to return. My absence would be noticed.

"Can we meet here again soon?" Cyfner wanted to learn more.

"My days do not belong to me, sir, but I shall try."

"I'm in the glade daily. It's here that I pray. I am among the last of the Druidic priests. Rome doesn't look kindly upon us."

"I shall do my best, sir. Thank you. I feel more composed. Thank you, sir."

Cyfner and I continued to meet. The old man explained that the Druidic code was simple. Three things are required of man—to worship the gods, do no evil, and maintain manly behaviour. I explained that was the same as the Golden Rule long taught in the East. The two of us had much to discuss, debate, and learn from each other. I thanked Yahweh for this.

The Rabbi was amused. *"You chose to follow me. Sometimes the journey is pleasant."*

At one meeting, Cyfner spoke of an event that had been troubling him for more than thirty years. Perhaps, since I had studied astronomy, I could shed some light on what he had seen in the night sky so long ago. Druids always sought knowledge and truth, but he recalled a star that didn't coincide with any of the calculations. His master-teacher hadn't been able to explain it; the star didn't appear on any of the astronomical charts.

Was I aware of such a phenomenon?

I was indeed! I told Cyfner that in Alexandria we had studied that very thing. Astronomers from Serica, I explained, a country thousands of miles farther east from Alexandria, had reported the sighting of a slow-moving star or comet in their skies during the later years of the reign of Caesar Augustus. These astronomers had reported that the star remained for more than seventy days—located in the sky's Capricorn region.

The Druid had seen this—and I had learned of this.

Cyfner pressed on. Did I know of this sighting's significance? Did it portend good or evil?

I could only explain myself by revealing what I had learned during my years in Israel, including what I had learned of their prophets and foretellings. I would have to reveal my years with the Rabbi, what I had witnessed and what I knew.

It was, however, springtime, which meant the resumption of carpentry—and with it, accidents.

It was also the time of birthing.

My services were in greater demand, consequently I had fewer opportunities to visit the glade.

Still, we met.

Cyfner told me that his long-ago master had taught him that human sacrifice was not what the All-Power required of the Druidic priests, because a king would be born who would appease the great god for man's iniquities in an act of pure sacrifice. His students, Cyfner among them, had dismissed this idea as the rantings of an old man; no one person's life could accomplish such a thing—to atone for all of mankind's sins.

However, in his old age and with our chance meeting, it now seemed that his master's words rang true.

Through our discussions, I noticed rales in my friend's breathing. Cyfner was aged, and such symptoms were not unexpected amongst the elderly.

One day I was called to Cyfner's dwelling, for he was dying. We both recognized the signs.

"My friend, you came," he said, propped up by pillows and still quite lucid.

"Of course, master."

"I'm not afraid, I go on…" Cyfner coughed and gasped.

"Yes, master, this journey ends. But a new one begins."

He smiled. "It has been my life's mission to find truth. How strangely bizarre, our meeting. Two different worlds… and through the All-Power's hand you have explained the one thing that has haunted me my entire life—that star. I have found meaning in my long-ago instructor's words. You, from far away, brought those words to the glade that day."

"Yes, master. As illogical a meeting as it was, it now appears to have been so very logical."

He was at peace.

I attended the secret Druidic burial and thanked Yahweh for allowing me the privilege to meet, share, and learn from this wise, curious-to-the-end soul.

It was a very large calf—and not only that, but the heifer's firstborn. I had been summoned, since a body is a body. My arms ached and there was blood everywhere, but with the aid of ropes, using the barn's uprights for leverage, the calf had been pulled into the world and resuscitated.

I washed as best I could and returned to base. The sentry laughed when I arrived, not unkindly, as my tunic was covered in splattered blood. I was dishevelled.

"You've been to a butchering?" the sentry asked.

"No, sir, a very messy delivery."

"Successful?"

"Yes, sir."

I fetched water and returned to the infirmary to cleanse and change into a fresh tunic.

"Now that's a sparrow of a different feather!" a woman said.

At her hearty laugh, I turned and found myself looking at Salome and Mary Magdelene. What were they doing here?

"What have you been up to?" Mary asked with a bright smile on her lips.

Behind the women was a gentleman I didn't recognize. They were also accompanied by the base's legate.

I had no chance to respond, for Salome's arms were already embracing me. She gave me a huge hug, as big as her laugh.

"We have missed you so!" Salome gushed.

Mary then introduced the gentleman. He wore fine clothing and kept his hair and beard according to the Jewish tradition.

"Darius, this is Joseph of Arimathea," Mary said. "The one who provided the Rabbi's tomb."

Joseph wasn't only freeborn but a man of importance. As for me, I was blood-splattered.

"Sir," I said to him with my head and eyes lowered.

The legate suggested that the guests go with him to the officers' hall while I prepared myself.

"Thank you, sir," I said, again following proper protocol.

Truly, what were they doing here?

Even my hair was tinged with red. It had been such a difficult birthing, but exhausted or not, I had visitors!

The centurions, optios, and kitchen staff were equally excited about my guests, eager for any news of the empire. Joseph was a man of business and everyone clung to his words.

I suddenly felt a kick. Then another! Across the table, I saw Salome flash a wicked smile... then she kicked me again. She was doing it under the table—deliberately!

I nudged her back. What else could I do?

She kicked again—

"What are you two doing?" Mary demanded. "If you're going to conduct yourselves like children, you shall both be sent from the table!"

My face reddened as I felt the blood flow to my face.

Salome let out a hearty laugh! "I did it. I made Darius redden. I win the bet. You owe me ten denarii."

The two ladies laughed. Levity! Oh how I had missed levity.

Joseph explained that he was on his way to Britannia on a trading mission. He exchanged Gallic wine, iron, tin, bronze mirrors, olive oil for their terra cotta bowls, and intricately crafted brooches and combs made from antlers. Mary and Salome were his dear friends and together they'd landed at Gesoriacum and taken a side trip to visit Darius. After a day or two, the group planned to return to the port and travel on to Britannia.

I was indeed delighted to see both Salome and Mary! But I was also uncomfortable sitting at the table with them—since they were all freeborn, all important in their own way, they were well above my station.

I kept my eyes lowered, quiet.

"How is it you know this physician?" the legate asked Joseph. "You must highly regard him to make a side trip to Vetera."

Joseph explained that he had only got to know me through my writings regarding Jesus of Nazareth.

The legate turned to me in surprise. "You're the scribe who chronicled the adventures of the Rabbi?"

"Yes, sir."

"You never mentioned that."

"You never asked, sir."

"Are the accounts true? We followed those reports. They were a welcome diversion."

Salome sensed my discomfort. "I have known Sparrow for a very long time, since he first came to Israel and was posted in Jerusalem. There is one thing about him you should know: he is incapable of deceit. It's just how his brain works. I can vouch for his honesty. Mary and I also witnessed everything Darius saw and reported. It's all true. Darius is a good scribe."

Fortunately, the serving girl quickly appeared with sweets and Joseph changed the nature of the conversation to matters of local agriculture. We left the men to talk of grain prices and border unrest.

I sat with the women outside the infirmary, our backs to the wall. I was positioned in the middle, with Salome and Mary each resting their heads on my shoulders. It was pleasant.

"We have missed you." Mary sighed. "Claudia was furious when she found out what Pilate had done."

"It was for the best, my lady."

"It's so very different here!" Salome said. "Where are the palm trees and desert sands? And the cook—she needs help!"

Mary and I both smiled.

"Claudia has sent you a few things," Mary said, opening her bag. "Tea all the way from Serica, pomegranates and nuts from Israel… and Olivia has made this for you." She handed me a clay oyster she had crafted. The shell was partly open to expose a pearl inside.

Mary spoke of events in Israel. The persecutions had continued, but they didn't come from Saul. This man who had terrorized the Rabbi's followers had recently fallen from his horse and been blinded. A voice had asked him why he was imprisoning the Rabbi's followers. Then he had been taken to Peter, where his sight was restored. Saul was now a believer and had changed his name to Paul. Many people still feared him, though.

The apostles and disciples had begun spreading the good news. Claudia had opened a home for widows and orphans in Joppa. Little

Simon had become quite the fisherman; Peter was now able to spend more time shepherding the flock, knowing that his son was providing for the family.

Olivia was helping Mother Mary and the other women tend to the needy in and around Jerusalem. Lazarus, Martha, and Mary were doing the same in Bethany, although Joseph of Arimathea was keen on having them relocate to Britannia with him as Lazarus had faced assassination attempts.

As for Joseph himself, he was seriously thinking of moving his family to Britannia, in fear that the persecution would only intensify.

"You look tired, Darius," Mary said after they'd given me all these updates. She sounded concerned. "Your eyes look different. Are you okay? Are you content?"

"I am, my lady. It was a difficult day. It's simply the demands of the job. I see too much disease, too much sadness, too many deaths. It was much easier being a scribe."

The three of us sighed.

"The Rabbi was a skilled carpenter," I added. "His life would have been so different if he had remained so."

"True, but that was not his calling, not the journey he was destined for," Salome reminded me. "It would have been easier, perhaps, to be a carpenter, but his mission was to redeem."

We let out another collective sigh, each of us lost in our own thoughts.

"There are so many hungry, so many homeless," Mary spoke. "Feed the hungry. Shelter the homeless. That's what the Rabbi told us to do, but it seems an impossible task! There are just too many hungry, too many in need."

"The Rabbi himself did not heal every sick person in Israel," I pointed out. "Just those he encountered."

Mary smiled at me. "I miss your logic."

"And I miss seeing you redden," Salome said to me with a chuckle. "Seriously, I suspect the two of you are burned out. The Rabbi would take a break when he was overwhelmed. I suggest that Mary and I remain here. Who wants to see Britannia? I would delight in teaching that cook a thing or two. Mary, you might pick up a few pointers from Sparrow to help you in treating illnesses in Jerusalem. Darius, having company would be as good as a rest."

"What a splendid idea, Salome!" Mary brightened. "We can meet up with Joseph after he returns from his trading mission. What do you think, Darius?"

"My lady, it is hardly a decision I could possibly make."

Salome's idea was interesting. The logistics, though… was this even possible?

"Well, I shall speak with the legate," Mary declared.

Mary squeezed my hand; Salome, the other. It was not unpleasant.

Another collective sigh. We were three unlikely friends, one a proper Jewish wife whose laughter could brighten the darkest chamber, one a former prostitute still of great beauty who now desired only to follow the Rabbi's teachings, and one a slaveborn physician who wished to be a scribe. We sat as allies, backs against the wall of a fort on the northern fringes of the empire. Each of our journeys was unique, each freely chosen.

We were connected by each one's decision to follow a Power who opted for redemption rather than annihilation. A Father who chose to send a part of Himself, His Son. A Son, trained as a carpenter, who chose a wooden cross to restore justice and harmony. It had been a pure sacrifice.

The Rabbi smiled down at these unlikely friends, wishing shalom upon them—peace to the hearts of those who had chosen wisely. Actions had consequences. The Shepherd knew His flock.

PART FIVE
The Sparrow Flies

M y second winter in northern Gaul was brutal. I had never seen snow or sleet or felt hail—and the novelty soon wore off! Everyone, including the horses, had to be draped in oilskin and fur. The services literally ground to a halt as the dirt roads became impassable; even the efficient Roman couriers couldn't get through. The conditions were unfit for man or beast.

Fever raged among the troops and locals alike. I did my best, but sadly there were deaths. When the medicinals ran low, I tried to befriend the local doulah, hoping to learn of the area's healing herbs, but she too succumbed before she could share her knowledge.

I was desperate to locate new healing plants, and I had a source: Cyfner's drawings of native healing plants. The wise old Druidic priest had gifted them to me before his death. I had noted each one's healing capabilities, where they were most likely to be found, and a more detailed physical description of each. I determined to seek these out, for I had patients to care for. I was indeed now a physician.

I didn't want to be a physician, though. I preferred life as a scribe.

"And I was content being a carpenter," said the Rabbi.

"Quit moping and move!" said Lucien.

The optio in the legate's office thought my mission was mad, but he conferred with his superior. Soon I was given permission to leave the base in search of these plants.

When I left, the sentry also thought my quest was insane. Still, he wished me good fortune as I set out in the freezing rain.

I was "away" while I walked. The weather became no matter as I examined leaves and stems and dug up roots with the knife I'd been given by the quartermaster. Armed with Cyfner's drawings, I gathered any plant I hoped might be useful.

As I worked, Lucien in my head instructed me in ways to determine each plant's safety. I was to rub it on my bare skin and watch for a rash, redness or burning sensation. Then I placed a tiny sample on my lip and waited to experience any negative sensations, such as heat and burning. At last I tasted a sample, placing it on the tongue, and again waited for symptoms. In some cases, I swallowed a tiny amount. Heat? Pain? Swelling?

So many times I experienced sores on my arms, lips, tongue, and throat. But I was "away," absorbed in my search.

I felt a sudden and unexpected thrust, but the blade didn't penetrate my raingear. I also heard a voice, a dialect with which I was unfamiliar. But since many dialects share words with each other, I could at least make out the command.

"Stand!"

The voice ordered me to stand.

Breathe, calm, focus. This time I added to my mantra: *Yahweh, help!*

Once I stood, my assailant tied my hands behind my back! I was his prisoner.

"Please, sir, my bags?" I said, using the dialect I'd learned from Cyfner. I hoped he would understand. "Please don't leave them… they're full of important roots and leaves."

The man seemed to understand. I saw his arm reach down and pick up the bags.

"Thank you, sir," I said.

And thank You, Yahweh.

My captor led me to a small encampment comprised of six oddly shaped conical tents. No one was visible outside in the inclement weather. I was placed in one that was empty, although a fire had been set in the middle; smoke exited through a hole in the structure's highest point.

"Sit," my captor ordered.

I obeyed.

I waited for some time, and the man eventually returned. He was not alone.

I felt it proper to stand, even though neither of them ordered me. These were freeborn. I had no idea of the proper protocol in such situations.

The newcomer approached me and pulled back the hood of my robe. He seemed to be in command, judging from his clothing, which was far more luxurious than that worn by the others.

"Who are you?" he demanded, looking at me closely. "Where do you come from? Why have you intruded on our territory?"

Just how far had I wandered? Had I crossed into Germania?

"I am Darius, sir, the physician for the Roman fort at Vetera," I said, feeling unsettled. "I was gathering herbs, roots, leaves, and healing plants, as the supplies in my dispensary are running low. There is much illness among the soldiers and locals. I didn't mean to trespass."

I didn't know whether this man could even understand me.

Breathe, calm, focus.

The leader left, leaving me alone with the one who had captured me. We stood in silence for several minutes.

Moments later, the leader returned with a third man. His robe was long, as was his beard. He also studied me closely.

"You are a Druid?" this man asked.

"No, sir."

"You speak their tongue. And you have these…"

He took out some of the drawings Cyfner had made for me. Obviously my captor had shown them to him.

"Yes, sir. These belonged to Cyfner, my friend. He gifted them to me before he died. He was a Druidic priest. I am but a slave."

"I thought you looked familiar. You were at the Great One's funeral. You are the yellow-haired physician."

"Yes, sir." It seemed these men remembered Cyfner as the Great One.

I was told to sit, after which everyone left.

But I wasn't alone for long, for a young woman soon entered. I was about to stand when she smiled and motioned for me to sit back down. She had brought me something to drink.

"Thank you, mistress."

She untied my ropes and then left.

I sniffed the liquid and found that the scent was unfamiliar. I decided not to drink it, even though the warm beverage seemed so welcoming.

When I paid attention, I heard voices speaking outside the shelter. One belonged to a young woman, perhaps the one who had brought the beverage. Then a man spoke. Was it her father?

"Can I keep him?" asked the woman. "He's pretty and he talks pretty."

"He's not a stray dog. He's from Vetera. This is a serious matter, girl…"

The voices faded.

No, I am not a stray, I thought. *I am owned by the emperor. I am an asset. If I fail to return to base, trackers will be on my trail. They will find this place. There will be a confrontation. There will be deaths.*

I closed my eyes and prayed.

Please, Lord Yahweh, let there be no more deaths because of me… not another incident. It's all my fault! I should have been careful. I should have been paying attention…

The others soon returned. It turned out that they had convened and decided to return me to the border.

The one who had also attended Cyfner's funeral emphasized how highly valued I must have been to that Druidic priest. In deference to Cyfner, they had decided that I should not be harmed.

Thank you, Cyfner. Thank you, Rabbi.

"Before you are returned to the border, are you not from the north?" inquired the leader. "Do you come from a part of Germania? What of your hair? Your colouring?"

"No, sir," I replied, my eyes and head lowered, as was the proper protocol; he was the leader. "I was born in Italia… Tuscany, sir."

When I returned to base, the hour was very late. The sentry remarked that they had begun to worry.

"Thank you, sir, but I am fine." I felt it unwise to say more.

I dried the plants, then compounded them according to the instructions I had recorded as Cyfner spoke. The new powders helped ease the spasms of coughing.

I had extra patients too, as the local herbalist had died early into the illness and more locals were seeking my assistance. This required me to go on more forays seeking out plants, roots, and herbs. On these occasions, I was more aware of my surroundings. Sometimes Natilis was assigned to protect me, if the patrols suspected border incursions. He still persisted in calling me "sir." That vexed me, but it was a comfort to know an armed guard was nearby.

One evening I stood in the doorway between the infirmary and my cell. I was about to retire when it suddenly hit me! I felt not just content; it was more than that. I felt *happy*.

The sick were sleeping soundly and I heard no coughing, gasping, or wheezing. There had been deaths, but not that many. Thank You, Yahweh! Was this why I was experiencing this new feeling? What had changed? Analysis was required.

I remembered a story the Rabbi had once told about a master who gave each of his slaves money to protect and perhaps grow during his absence. Was I the foolish servant? Had I been burying my talent?

My logical brain deduced that I couldn't change the circumstances into which I'd been born, nor could I change my physical mien or the quirks in my personality that caused others annoyance. These were not of my choosing.

What I did have was a brilliant mind and facility to learn.

Had I been hiding, burying my talent behind a desk, content and safe to keep translating, transcribing, and recording?

Teaching the children had been pleasant, affording a sense of accomplishment in knowing that my charges had a basic knowledge of Latin and Greek, and that those preparing for their bar and bat mitzvahs were proficient in reading Hebrew scriptures.

Was I happy now as a physician because I was using my full potential to help others despite my phobias and obsessions? Had I accepted that my journey wasn't all about me but rather about helping those most in need? Is that why I was happy?

"It took him long enough!" said Lucien.

The Rabbi chimed in: *"Such brains, they require more time."*

Spring mercifully came early. The sick recovered and the fort returned to normal.

I enjoyed writing letters for the soldiers—and the courier sometimes brought replies! It must have been a comfort for them to know that someone awaited their return. Those who received mail would eagerly seek me out! I gladly read these letters to eager ears, and their fellow soldiers rejoiced in hearing a comrade's news from home.

Natilis wore me down over time, and eventually I did admit that I was the scribe who had accompanied the Rabbi and reported on his activities. I read my reports to him and his friends and answered their questions. I feared I'd be ridiculed, but I wasn't. The soldiers appeared awed. I felt humble.

The officers were more sceptical, much like the woman long ago—it felt so very long ago—who had questioned my integrity in Jerusalem. They wondered how anyone could forgive those who had driven nails through his flesh and suspended him for three hours to die horrifically?

Rabbi had used stories of seeds, weeds, and reaping—after all, he had been speaking to a rural audience. But before me now were professional military men, so I used a word they could relate to: mission.

"It was his mission," I said, hoping they would understand. "He willingly accepted this assignment, sirs."

It was difficult to speak with people about the Rabbi's message. I felt that it wasn't my place.

"I am not trained in these matters," I told the Rabbi one evening.

"Really?" he replied.

It had been a long day with many patients and many procedures, on and off base, both human and animal. To me, a body was a body, like a machine, with the same working parts.

I was unusually tired that night and slept soundly

I felt a nudge!

"Wake up, Sponge!"

My eyes snapped open at the sound of Lucien's voice.

"Come, many are awaiting your arrival," my mentor said. "Move!"

And the Rabbi was near as well: "Come, Darius. We heard you asking for death to come quick, if it came."

But I wasn't afraid; I was unsettled.

"Master?" I asked. "Is this the terminus of my journey?"

"It is," said the Rabbi. "You have planted the seeds, my friend. You have been a good and faithful servant. But there are changes ahead. The Roman Empire is in decline. The new Caesars will be consumed by both power and greed. Caligula will choose to scapegoat my followers. There will be much upheaval, much torture, and many martyrdoms. You, Sparrow, will be spared. You are, after all, 'not brave.'"

Was that levity?

"Many are waiting," Lucien said.

"Indeed. Come my friend, into my Father's kingdom."

I hesitated. "No, Rabbi, I cannot."

The Rabbi smiled, but Lucien appeared annoyed.

"Are you defying an order?" the Rabbi asked with a grin.

"No, sir. Rather I'm deferring one. I cannot go with you. I am not worthy. Because I doubted." I kept my eyes and head lowered as required.

"To doubt is totally *human*. It's normal to doubt, Sparrow. Before you test a new hypothesis, do you not have doubt that it will prove true? When you administer a new herbal or medicinal, do you not question whether it will be effective? Yet you do not abandon your theory or discard the drug. It is human to doubt, Sparrow. It reminds humans they are not... well, me!" The Rabbi smiled broadly. "It is what one does next that reveals what is in one's heart... the wonder of Yahweh, giving humans the gift of free choice. Will doubt lead to disillusionment, to despair? Or will doubt lead to a leap of faith? You doubted my resurrection—at first. But you accepted. You proclaimed it when prodded."

"But, sir, you marked me. That pinch remained to remind me of my failures. I am not worthy to enter your kingdom."

Lucien spoke up. "He was never one to be able to unlock a metaphor, even if he held the key in his hand."

"Darius." The Rabbi's voice was kind. "Did you never consider its location?"

"Location, Rabbi?" I was confused.

"I feared he couldn't find his way out of a grain sack." Lucien laughed. "Such a brain, yet so obtuse!"

"The mark, Sparrow! I placed it *above* the mark of Augustus. Above the earthly realm that claimed you. Yahweh's kingdom is above man's; that's what the pinch mark symbolized. Sparrow, that wasn't a mark of shame. It was a reminder of the truth."

I didn't know what to say.

Lucien shook his head.

The Rabbi laughed. "Come, Sparrow, many are waiting for your arrival. You have earned your inheritance, my brother."

A sparrow! Suddenly, I saw it—in the sky. Its brown feathers weren't drab but brilliant! Bronze, copper, gold…

The Rabbi smiled again. "Yahweh sees the value in even the lowly sparrow, Sparrow."

The door to my room opened and Natilis peered inside.

"Sir, the cook said that you'd not come for your morning tea so I brought it to you before I go on duty… sir?"

Natilis dropped the cup, the contents splashing over the floor.

When his fellow soldiers heard the noise, they too entered the room. The legate was among them.

"Sir's dead!" Natalis said in shock.

"He looks so…" The legate seemed at a loss for words. "What was the word the physician would use when offered barley beer or sour wine?"

"Content."

"Yes, he looks *content.*"

"That's odd," said Natalis. "The figurine of the sparrow is missing. Sir had two of them, both gifts—a sparrow and an oyster. The sparrow... it's gone."

The legate arranged for a funeral far above that which was normally reserved for a mere slave. Many villagers came, and the children brought flowers.

No one noticed the long-robed figure standing apart amongst the trees.

If Master Cyfner, the Deon, valued the physician, there must be truth in his words, thought the young Druid-in-training. He had felt the need to attend the yellow-haired one's funeral, just as Darius had attended Cyfner's.

All watched as one of the soldiers affixed the figurine of an oyster to the large rock that was placed over the grave.

As the mourners drifted away, Natilis remained. The young soldier needed a bit more time, alone, to say his farewells to Sir.

Unexpectedly, a small brown sparrow fluttered by and came to a rest upon the figurine of the oyster.

In that same moment, Natalis heard a voice in his head. It was Sir.

"Yahweh sees the value in even the lowly sparrow, sir."

The soldier smiled. "Indeed He does."